Murder With a Sliver of Cake

An Ivy Clark Mystery

Kristy T Dixon

Chapter 1

"It looks perfect!" I said, looking at the white layered cake José and Carrie had just finished decorating.

José frowned. "I don't know. It's missing something."

"That's what you say every time." Carrie stretched her back.

The cake was excellent, and all the other attempts were, too. José was being picky.

"It's my wedding, and I say this is the one," I said. "Let me text Jett and see if he can run by."

José studied the cake. "It might be too small."

"No, it's great. Any bigger, and it will be impossible to move."

Carrie nodded. "I keep telling him that. We don't want to bring it in on a forklift."

I pulled out my phone and sent a text. Our wedding was in a week, and everything was finally coming together after postponing for Jett's dad's emergency surgery. Now he was recovered, the weather was warmer, and things felt... almost too perfect.

"I'm not sure it's going to taste right," José worried.

Carrie glared at him. "It will taste just fine."

I smiled and went to the front doors of my diner to make sure Jett could get in. We were closed for the evening, and I'd probably locked the doors. I could hear Carrie and José still discussing the cake in the kitchen. They had gotten married a few months ago, so I hoped the cake wasn't causing their first fight.

Muddy Creek is a small town, so it was likely that wherever Jett was, it wasn't far. He should be off duty and probably home.

I opened the door and jumped when Jett was already standing there. "Whoa!"

He grinned. "I was just down the street when you texted me. Cake?"

I nodded. "José isn't happy with it, but I think it's the best one."

"José is too much of a perfectionist."

We went back to the kitchen to find Carrie with her hands on her hips, giving him a lecture.

"Looks great," Jett said, cutting her off. "That's the one we want. No arguing."

José sighed. "Fine. But taste it before you decide." He cut four pieces, and we all sat at the island and took a bite.

"Okay," José admitted. "That tastes great."

I smiled. It really did, and I was glad José was happy with it. The taste, anyway.

We ate cake and talked for a while, then cleaned up. Everyone in town was probably sick of wedding cake by now—we'd been giving it away free at the diner the day after each of José's experiments.

"The last cake I made, Opal came over and measured the tiers to see if they were even." José frowned. "Of course, they weren't exact, and she was all too happy to tell me about it."

"Opal's just like that," I said. "Don't let her worry you. It looks great."

"It does," Carrie agreed. "And if you don't stop making cakes every day, you're going to go crazy."

José stood. "Don't you think the icing might be a little... thin?"

"It's not thin," Jett assured him. "You're just looking for problems. We aren't picky, and even if we were, it looks great."

"I suppose."

"Come on." Carrie stood. "I'm tired."

After José and Carrie left, Jett followed me upstairs to my apartment. I live above the diner, with a staircase inside and another out back. This door went to my room, then we went from there into my living room.

Creepers ran over, rubbing against my ankles.

"Hey," I said, scooping him up and rubbing his soft gray fur. "Did you miss me?"

He meowed, and I sat on the couch. Jett dropped down beside me and propped his feet on the coffee table.

"Long day?" I asked.

"Not too bad. Ledford's about to drive me crazy with all his geocaching talk. I can't wait until he finishes it."

Jett was the sheriff of Muddy Creek, and Ledford was one of his deputies. Ledford was setting up a huge town geocaching event—basically a giant Easter egg hunt on steroids—with clues. He'd been planning hiding spots for months. I was doubtful, but he swore it was my kind of thing.

I'd solved a few crimes in Muddy Creek, and I couldn't help but wonder if this was his way of trying to keep me out of his cases.

The doorbell rang, and I groaned. It was after ten, and I was ready to go to bed. That bell meant someone was at the diner's front door. Anyone I knew would come to my apartment entrance.

"Ignore it," Jett said, draping an arm over my shoulders.

I leaned against him and closed my eyes.

The bell rang again.

"What if it's an emergency?" I asked.

"They can come around back."

"It feels like things are always so busy. I hate the door-bell." I tilted my head and kissed him lightly. I couldn't believe how much my life had changed in less than two years. I'd relocated from Arizona to Kansas, taken over my late grandma's diner... and then there was Jett. He made the hard times worth it.

A sharp pounding sounded on my front door. My stomach tightened. Maybe it was an emergency. I stood, a little nervous about who might be there.

"I'll get it." Jett stood and crossed the room, then pulled open the door.

I gasped. My cousin Tania stood there. Last I'd heard, she was still in prison.

Her eyes narrowed at Jett, though I couldn't tell if it was because he was here or because the light from the apartment was in her face.

Jett stepped back. "Hey, Tania. It's been a while."

I pasted on a smile that felt more like a lie. The last time I'd seen her was when I testified against her in court. The time before that, I'd tackled her when she tried to escape Jett. Awkward didn't even begin to cover the feel of the room.

"Hi, Tania." I hoped she wasn't here to kill me or anything.

She stepped in, lips tightening as she glanced around. "You added to the place."

I nodded. When I'd first moved in, it had been just a room and a small bathroom. Now it was a two-bedroom apartment.

"Sit," I offered, not sure what else to say.

She dropped onto the couch—right in the middle. That made things worse. The only other seat was the recliner, and while I didn't want to sit next to Tania, I wanted Jett to sit by her even less.

Jett leaned against the wall beside the recliner, arms crossed. I sat in the recliner and faced my cousin.

"How are you?" I finally asked.

She shrugged. "As good as I can be."

"Good. Uh... when did you..." I was unsure how to ask.

"I got released this morning."

"Ah."

"I know you don't want to see me, but I don't have anywhere to go. Mom's going to be in prison for life, and now I have no house to go to. I'm guessing you sold Uncle Rob's house?"

I nodded.

"I figure you pretty much took everything from me, so the least you can do is let me stay with you for a while."

My eyes narrowed. "Really? Took everything from you?"

"Yeah. This place should be mine, and so should part of Rob's house."

"This place is mine because of Gramma Sue's will. I would have let you have it since your mom ran it, but you made some bad choices."

She leaned forward, shoulder-length black hair falling across her face. "Maybe, but now I'm left with nothing."

"I set up a trust for you."

She blinked. "Really?"

I nodded. "With your part of the sale of Uncle Rob's house and the complete sale of your mom's house."

She chewed her lip and, for once, looked a little ashamed. "Thanks."

I nodded.

"Can I stay with you until I figure things out?"

I sighed. Who knew how long that would take? And I didn't trust her. I looked up at Jett, and he came over to perch on the armrest of my chair.

"For how long?" he asked.

Tania glared at him. "How should I know? And what does it matter to you? This is a family matter, not a law matter."

"I'll be family in a week, and then I'll live here, so yeah—it affects me."

She scowled. "You two are getting married?"

"Yep."

Tania had always made me second-guess myself, but I wasn't going to let her start intimidating me again.

"You should be able to access the money immediately," I said. "I do have an extra room, but I'd need you out in five or six days." I could let her stay while we were on our honeymoon, but I didn't trust her.

"Alright. Thanks. I haven't eaten since breakfast. Do you have anything I can have?"

"Of course." I stood and headed toward the kitchen. "Follow me." I fixed her a sandwich, then left her eating alone.

Jett was on the recliner with Creepers curled in his lap. I lifted the cat and settled on Jett.

"Is this okay?" I whispered.

He kissed my forehead, frowning. "I don't want you alone with her."

"Neither do I."

"I'm staying on the couch."

"You don't have to—"

"I'll be stressed otherwise. You're part of the reason she got arrested, and she might hold a grudge."

"You were another part of the reason."

"I have a gun."

I smiled and shook my head. "That doesn't make you invincible."

"No, but better with it than without."

I wasn't sure what I would do with Tania tomorrow. She knew how to run the diner, but I wasn't sure I wanted her there. I didn't want her up here with Creepers all day either.

Tania came out, almost disguising a glare. If she didn't like me sitting on Jett, she could go to the B&B. She'd liked him at one point, so who knew what was running through her head.

"I'm too tired to eat much. Where am I staying?" she asked.

I stood, handed Creepers to Jett, and led her to the guest room. She set her purse on the bed and glanced around.

"I can't believe you're marrying Jett. It's so... unexpected. You know we dated, right?"

"I know you went on one date. I don't count that as dating."

"Yeah, whatever. He isn't my type," she lied.

"He has some deputies now. Some are pretty good looking." I didn't know why I was saying that. I wouldn't sic Tania on anyone I liked.

Her eyes lit up. "Oh yeah?"

"Yep. I should introduce you to Ledford." It would kind of serve them both right.

"What's he like?"

"Super strong, brown hair. Comes off annoying but grows on you."

"Hmm."

"Let me know if you need anything."

"Thanks. And Ivy? I really am sorry. I only did everything I did to protect my mom."

"I know." Not that it made it right.

I went back out to find Jett already half asleep on the couch with Creepers sprawled across his chest.

"Is Creepers growing on you?" I asked. Jett wasn't against cats, but they weren't exactly on his list of favorites.

"Like a fungus," he muttered.

I scooped up the cat and carried him to my room, then grabbed a pillow and blanket for Jett. I was sure that within a month, the two of them would be best friends.

Chapter 2

"Who let the dogs out?" Barbra yelled out with the music.

I smiled as I kicked my leg into the air in what I hoped was an amazing Zumba move. I watched my class move around and thought back to my first time teaching in Muddy Creek. My students had come a long way. Most of them were over fifty. And by most, I mean all.

Opal jumped up, then down. She'd been most skeptical when the class started and spent several classes grumbling, and now she was better than everyone but Barbra.

Boyd was doing his own thing. Not that it was surprising. I'd thought he would quit coming when he became mayor, but it wasn't as much work as I'd imagined. He knocked into his neighbor, who rolled her eyes and moved farther away.

Tania stood in the back, filming with her phone. I did my best to ignore the way she posed with it like she was on a stage. I wasn't sure why she'd come, but if she was trying to move her life in a better direction, I certainly wasn't going to stop her.

Boyd collided with Barbra, and they both toppled. The music blasted on, and Boyd, flat on the floor, rolled over like he was making snow angels. "I call that move the Mayor Shuffle."

Barbra huffed, pulling herself up. "Goodness, Boyd. Watch what you're doing."

"Sorry," he said, grinning as two women hauled him to his feet.

When I'd first certified to teach Zumba, I'd pictured a sleek gym, mirrors on the walls, and neon-clad twenty-somethings flipping their hair. Instead, I had Boyd inventing new moves, Barbra commanding the playlist, and Opal outdancing everyone else. And somehow—I loved it. These were my people.

The music pounded so loud the floor shook, sneakers squeaked, and the room smelled like a mix of sweat and flowery Bath & Body Works lotion.

Barbra fixed her messy pink ponytail and kept dancing. We used to stop the music whenever someone went down, but we'd voted and everyone wanted it to keep going. No one wanted all the attention on them when they fell.

Class ended, and I flipped off the music and watched everyone trickle out.

"Thanks, hon," Barbra said, wiping her forehead on a towel. "I don't know how we survived before you came to town."

Tania frowned from her place in the back.

I smiled. "Thanks for coming, Barbra."

"I love it."

Soon, it was just Tania and me, and the awkwardness that comes with sending your cousin to prison.

"I'm surprised you kept up the class," Tania said, straightening her pink tank top.

"I miss a lot, but no one seems to mind."

Jett burst through the door, and passed Tania without seeing her. "I'm off duty," he said. "Ready to go try on my tux?" He wrapped his arms around my waist and picked me up.

"Gross. Put me down," I protested. "I'm all sweaty and smelly."

"I love you no matter how you smell."

He let me slide to my feet, then kissed me.

"Come on," Tania muttered.

Jett glanced casually over his shoulder. "Oh, hey, Tania."

"Let me go shower, then we can go," I said.

"Alright, but the shop closes at noon."

"I'll hurry."

Thirty minutes later, I was in Jett's truck, and we were driving to the city. Somehow, Boyd had convinced Jett to let him come, and he was in the back talking about Zumba and everything else that crossed his mind.

After fifteen minutes, he ran out of things to say, and five minutes later, he was softly snoring.

Jett had a slight smile on his face. "I guess he wore himself out."

I laughed. "You should have seen him in Zumba today. He was crazy. He knocked Barbra over."

"Ooh. Not surprising, but I'm sure she wasn't happy."

"I'm shocked no one's broken anything with how many falls we've had."

"How's your diner doing lately? You haven't been spending a lot of time in the kitchen."

"It's fine. They usually don't need me. I think José likes feeling in charge, and when I'm there, it throws him off his groove."

"I can see that."

We pulled into the city and weaved around until we came to the small shop where Jett wanted to rent a tux. Boyd woke up, and we went inside.

The shop had polished wood floors that gleamed like someone had just buffed them and walls lined with tuxedos in shades of black and navy that looked like they belonged in magazines. A faint smell of cologne lingered in the air, like the store itself had spritzed on aftershave for our arrival.

The man at the counter turned to us and sighed. "Can I help you?"

"We have an appointment," Jett told him. "Jett Malone."

The man sighed again, then came out and led us to the back of the room. "These are probably the ones you want to look at," he said. "More in your price range."

My eyes narrowed, and I studied Jett. He was in his casual clothes, which consisted of faded jeans and a black button-up shirt. His look didn't scream "money," but it didn't scream "destitute," either. Then there was Boyd in his Hawaiian shirt and sweatpants. Something I could only call retired tourist chic.

"I didn't tell you my price range," Jett said.

"Fine," the man said. "But you might as well start here."

"I'd look good in this stuff," Boyd said, touching a tux. The salesman sucked in a breath, as if he was afraid Boyd might make the tuxes worth less.

"I'm going to have to ask you not to touch," he said.

Boyd looked at him. "Then how do we know what we like?"

"Just tell me what you want, and I'll get it down."

Jett's eyes scanned the racks. "They all look about the same."

The man visibly shuddered. "They are quite different. This is the cheapest rental," he said, taking one off the rack.

"Hmm," Jett said. "Not my style."

I smiled and shook my head. Jett had just admitted he thought they all looked the same, and I was sure he didn't really care what he got, but this guy was getting under his skin.

Boyd went over near a wall and took a pink bow tie from a stand. "What do you think?" he asked, holding it up to his Hawaiian shirt. "Classy casual. That's what I'd call it."

The salesman looked as if he might pass out.

I wondered what a salesperson here must make for them to be so high and mighty. I Googled it while Jett talked to the man. Hmm. Definitely not enough to be auditioning for Villain of the Year.

Boyd's phone rang, and he pulled it out. "Mayor Webster here." He moved over to the other side of the shop to finish the call.

"Did he just say 'mayor?'" the man asked.

I nodded. "He's the mayor of Muddy Creek."

"Interesting."

I bet it was.

"Yeah," I said. "You wouldn't know it from his outfit, but he's pretty well-to-do."

Jett gave me a *what-are-you-talking-about* look. Boyd does have money, but it's not like me to bring something like that up. Still, this guy was bugging me.

"Sheriff Malone?" Boyd said, handing Jett his phone. "It's Mr. Sims from the county. He has some questions you're more qualified to answer."

Jett took Boyd's phone and excused himself.

"You can show me the tuxes," I said. "He'll go with whatever I say anyway."

The man nodded and showed me a few. I'd say Jett was right. They all looked so similar, I couldn't say one was better than another.

"That one." I pointed at one of the middle-priced pieces. "Let's have him try it."

Jett returned and took the tux into the dressing room.

When he came out, I nearly forgot to breathe. "You look hot."

"That's because they have the heat on." Boyd waved his hand like a fan. "Kind of a waste of money in this weather."

"So, this one?" Jett asked me. "I don't want to try on more than I have to."

"I think so."

"What color bow tie?" the salesman asked.

"I don't care," Jett said, straightening the jacket.

"Blue," I said. We didn't have actual wedding colors, but Jett looked good in blue.

"Doesn't it look a little tight in the shoulders?" Boyd asked.

I smiled. "Maybe that's why I like it."

"Aren't you worried he might Hulk out of it in the middle of the ceremony?"

The salesman looked like he'd like to crawl under the counter. "Does it need any adjusting?" he asked.

"Nope," Jett said. "It's fine."

"Then change, and we can check out."

I wandered to the window and stared out at the street. Wedding preparations were tiring and not as exciting as they're made out to be.

A Levi's Auto Shop van pulled in across the street.

"Isn't that the auto shop in Muddy Creek?" I asked Boyd.

He squinted. "Yep. I wonder why they would come here. Wichita has its own shops. It wouldn't need anyone from our neck of the woods driving in."

A man got out and went to the back, then took out a twelve-inch box. He set it on the sidewalk, got in the van, and drove off.

"Odd place to deliver something," I said.

Boyd nodded.

A man walking down the street scooped up the box and kept walking.

"Drug deal?" I asked.

"Who knows?"

Jett came over and looked out. "What did you say?"

We told him what had happened.

"We aren't worrying about that. Not our town."

"But some of our people," Boyd said.

"It was probably nothing."

That was what Jett said, but I could see something in his eyes, and in the way his jaw tightened. Like he knew something and wasn't sharing.

Chapter 3

Jett had me pinned between the outside wall of the diner and him, and I had no intention of trying to get away. Boyd had gone upstairs to play with Creepers, and I think Jett was hitting his Boyd tolerance level.

"We're getting so close," he said. He kissed me softly, and my arms tightened around him.

"We should have gone to a different shop," I said. "That clerk was stuck up."

He kissed my cheek. "Yeah, but it was the closest one and had good reviews."

"I want to give it a bad one." Jett kept kissing my face, distracting me from the mean review I was trying to write in my head.

"Emergency!" Carol Malone said, rushing past us. "Upstairs, both of you."

I looked at Jett, and he shrugged.

Carol hurried up the steps with a heavy-looking garment bag in her hands.

We followed, and Jett leaned in to me. "Have you noticed how everyone wants to butt in when I'm trying to kiss you?"

I smiled. "It does seem that way sometimes."

We went into the apartment and found Boyd on the couch talking to Creepers.

"Hello, Carol," he greeted.

"We have a problem," she said, pulling two light-pink dresses from her bag. She held them side by side. "Look at this."

I looked at the dresses, wondering what she was getting at. She'd ordered a dress for her and one for my mom so they would match.

"They look nice."

"But look closer."

I squinted and looked at Jett.

"They look fine to me," he said.

"They aren't the same color!"

I blinked. "They look the same to me."

"Nope. One is slightly lighter."

Jett laughed. "Mom, they're fine. No one's going to notice."

"I hope not. It's too late to send one back, and who's to say they wouldn't just send another bad one?"

"Which one is the bad one?" Boyd asked.

"It doesn't matter. It just matters that they aren't the same. Look. One is a little washed out."

Boyd scanned the dresses. "Nope. Same."

I honestly couldn't see any difference either.

"Mom, no one cares." Jett placed his hand on her arm.

She looked at me. "Ivy?"

"I don't see a problem."

She let out a breath. "Oh good. I was worried you might be upset."

"No. I see people planning their weddings for years, just to make them perfect. They're always stressed, and it never goes as planned. I figure, plan fast and have fun. In the end, I want Jett. The rest is just details. If the cake sinks and the decorations all tip over, that's fine. I still get what's important."

Jett grinned and pulled me against him. "That is what I needed to hear." He kissed me in a way I wasn't totally comfortable with in front of his mom. And Boyd. But Boyd seemed to be everywhere, so he was hard to avoid.

"I think Boyd and I are going to go," Carol said.

I pulled away and glared at Jett. "You don't have to go."

"I'm going to call your mom. Just to make sure she's okay with this mess-up."

She hurried out the door, and Boyd followed her, already telling her some story he'd probably just made up.

"You can't kiss me like that in front of your mom."

"Why not?"

"It's embarrassing."

"Could have been worse."

"I doubt it."

"It could have been more like this." He dipped me, and I let out a shriek that they probably heard down in the diner.

"Don't scare the guests." He smiled down at me.

Jett kissed me, and my phone buzzed. He lifted me, and I pushed my hair back into place.

I grabbed my phone and looked at my text. "It's José. He made another cake."

"He needs to stop. He's made way too many."

"Yeah, he's going to be a professional before he's through."

"I guess we go down and taste it?"

"Sure," he said, taking my hand. We descended the stairs and found a cake that was much too big. Pretty, but ridiculous.

"That's too big," Jett said. "There's no way we could transfer it."

"Told you." Carrie rubbed her temples.

"I can make it smaller," José offered.

"It looks great, but I still like the one from yesterday," I said.

"Alright, alright. But don't blame me if it isn't everything you ever dreamed of. I'd hate to ruin the wedding."

I shook my head. "Why is everyone more stressed about this wedding than I am? Even if the cake fails, I won't blame you, and it will be fine." I wondered how much we'd spent on wedding cake ingredients this month.

I turned to Jett. "I wonder where Tania went. I just realized I haven't seen her since Zumba."

"I think she's embarrassed to see anyone," Carrie said. "She snuck down earlier and got some food, but then she went right back upstairs."

I groaned. That probably meant she was in the guest room listening to Jett and me and probably judging.

Jett winked at me, likely knowing exactly what I was thinking.

"Well, we can't waste the cake," José declared. "Everyone, get a plate."

I held in a deep sigh. I was almost sick of wedding cake, no matter how good José made it. We all ate a slice, and I took one up with Jett to give to Tania.

Jett sat on the couch, and I went to the guest room and knocked. "Tania?"

"Yeah?"

"Do you want a piece of cake?"

The door opened. "Sure. Thanks." She took it and shut the door. That was fine. I went back out to Jett and Creepers.

"Don't you want to go outside?" I asked my cat.

He just looked at me from his place on top of the couch.

"I'm staying here again," he said quietly.

"I don't think she's a threat."

"Maybe not, but she's always been unpredictable. Even when we were kids."

"What's she going to do?"

"I don't want to think about that, but she can't get to your room without passing the couch, so that's where I'm gonna be."

I grabbed the remote and flipped on the TV. If he wanted to sleep on the small couch, that was his choice. Tania might not be my favorite relative, but I doubted she would do anything. Unpredictable didn't mean dangerous. At least, that was what I told myself.

I fell asleep before the movie ended, and when I woke, it was dark outside. Jett was still watching something.

"What time is it?" I asked.

"About eleven."

"Sorry. I'll go to bed so you can sleep."

"I'm fine."

Tania came in and rolled her eyes. "Don't you have your own place?"

Jett smiled. "I do. How about you?"

She scowled. "I will."

"I figure I have more right to be here than you do."

She crossed her arms, and I seriously hoped there wasn't going to be a Jett/Tania clash.

"How do you figure? Ivy is my cousin, and my mom used to own this place."

"Yeah, but that changed, and your cousin relationship hasn't been warm and fuzzy."

"Maybe not, but family trumps relationships every time." She turned and stalked away. Those were some interesting words, considering our history. Tania had never put me ahead of anything in her life.

"Some people never change," Jett said.

"I'll get you a blanket."

A loud crash echoed up from the diner below.

Creepers's ears flattened, and he hissed.

My eyes flew to Jett.

Chapter 4

Jett was off the couch and halfway down the stairs before I could react. I bolted after him, hoping the noise was just a pan tipping over in the kitchen. My feet pounded down the steps, through the dining area, and into the kitchen—where I stopped short. I sucked in a breath. A man lay motionless on the floor. José's cake had collapsed across him in a mess of frosting and crumbs.

Jett was on his knees, pushing the cake off the man. It smelled like vanilla and the tire section of Walmart. He looked up at me. "Stay out. And call Ledford. This man's dead."

I cringed. "Why do these things keep happening around me?" I pulled out my phone and dialed Ledford.

"Hello?" he answered. "Ivy?"

"Yeah, uh, there's a dead guy in the diner kitchen. Jett's here, and he wants you to come."

He sighed. "On my way."

"He's coming," I told Jett.

"You shouldn't be in here."

"You know I'm not leaving. Who is it?" My stomach tightened, unsure if I really wanted to know.

"I don't know him. Do you?"

I glanced at the frosting-covered corpse—a man, maybe fifty, his face pale beneath streaks of buttercream. "No."

"Go tell Tania so she doesn't freak out and come down here."

"Okay." I figured he was trying to get me to go away, but it would only take a minute.

I ran upstairs and knocked on Tania's door.

"Come in!" she called.

I opened the door a crack. She sat on the bed, staring at her phone. "Something's going on in the diner. You might see cops and hear stuff."

"That explains the crash. What happened?"

"I'm not sure, but there's a dead guy."

Her eyes went wide. "Are we in danger?"

I hadn't thought of that.

"I'm not sure. I don't know how the guy died."

"Wow. That's two people dying in the diner since you came."

I gave her a tight smile. No point in correcting her. "Just stay up here and lock your door."

I headed back toward the kitchen. Without her fake lashes and nails, Tania looked... tired. I guess prison could do that to a person.

Ledford was at the front door, banging to be let in. I unlocked it, and he brushed past me without a word, heading straight for the kitchen. I followed.

"What do you need?" Ledford asked Jett.

Jett looked up. "Do you know him?"

Ledford crouched for a better look. "Elias Prescott. Just moved to town a month or so back. He works at the new auto body shop."

"Levi Calloway runs that?" Jett asked.

"Yeah. Any sign of what happened?"

"He's got a lump the size of a grapefruit on his head. I'm guessing frying pan." Jett nodded toward one of our big cast-iron pans.

I scanned the kitchen. "How'd he get in here? Nothing else looks disturbed." I walked to the back door. "It's unlocked."

"Did we forget to lock it, or did someone force it?" Jett joined me. "Doesn't look like it's been messed with."

I glanced up at him. "I hope I didn't forget."

He pulled on a glove and eased the door open. "Look here."

Scratches were scored on the outside of the doorframe. At least Elias Prescott wasn't dead in my kitchen because of something I did… or didn't do.

I bent down and pointed at a piece of twine in the dirt by the door. "Is this important?"

"Twine?" Jett asked. "Not sure."

Ledford came over, picked it up in his gloved hand, and frowned. "Could be tied to the case I'm working on."

Jett pulled a baggie from his pocket, and Ledford dropped it inside. Jett always had a baggie and a glove. They were like his calling card.

"If there was a scuffle down here, why didn't we hear it?" I asked.

Jett shut the door. "We might've been distracted and missed it when Tania was talking to us."

"I doubt it. It's hard to block out noise down here."

"Who's Tania?" Ledford asked.

"My cousin. She's upstairs." My eyes went wide. "What if she was distracting us from something down here?" Even I heard how ridiculous that sounded.

"Doubtful," Jett said. "She's been in prison. I don't think she'd suddenly be in on someone's scheme."

"Your cousin was in prison?" Ledford grinned. "You put her there?"

I shrugged. "Maybe."

"You did? I was joking."

I wrinkled my nose. "Shouldn't we be talking about the dead guy?"

"You should be in bed," Jett said. "We'll wait here for the paramedics."

I was tired, but I hated to miss anything.

"I'll let you know if anything happens, alright?"

"Fine," I muttered. "But only because I've been up forever."

I went upstairs, got ready for bed, and fell asleep like there wasn't a body in my diner.

The following morning, I was up early. Tania sat on the couch, she and Creepers giving each other the stink eye.

"You wanna go down to breakfast?" I asked. I didn't know what was going on downstairs, but I could smell bacon, so Jett must not have shut the diner down as a crime scene.

"I guess," Tania said. "I'm a little nervous to see people from town after what I did."

"It's a Tuesday. Probably not a lot of people. And you already went to Zumba."

"Yeah, but that's just the older population in town. I don't care what they think."

Typical Tania.

We went down the stairs and stopped at the bottom.

"Peek in and see how many people there are," Tania commanded.

I leaned around the corner. "Only Ledford," I said. "And he doesn't know you."

She peeked too. "Hmm. He's not bad looking... except for that awful mustache. I wonder if he'd shave."

I shook my head. Not even introduced, and she was already trying to change him.

"Maybe I should wait to meet him until I get my lashes done."

"You look fine."

She had more makeup on than yesterday, and her hair fell in loose curls to her shoulders. She was also wearing my clothes—but I wouldn't say anything. At least not this time.

"Come on," I urged.

Tania took a deep breath, and we walked into the dining area.

Ledford looked up and gave me a slight smile. Ledford and I had started badly, but weird experiences had made us... not friends, but not enemies either. His eyes shifted to Tania and bugged just slightly.

"Hey, Deputy Ledford," I said. "Can we sit with you?"

"Of course," he said—like he meant it, which wasn't his usual personality.

We sat across from him.

"This is my cousin, Tania. Tania, this is Deputy Ledford."

They shook hands and exchanged polite noises I didn't bother listening to. My mind was still on the dead man.

"So you're the jailbird?" Ledford asked.

I snapped back. "Seriously? Didn't your parents ever tell you not to say everything that crosses your mind?"

Tania sighed. "It's alright. I was in jail. My mom... was about to go to jail, and I panicked and tried to cover for her."

"I guess that's not as bad as some things," he said.

My eyes widened. That didn't sound like Ledford.

"I thought the diner would be closed," I said.

He shrugged. "We were up most of the night. Had a couple of forensics come in from Wichita."

"So that's why there was noise all night," Tania said.

I didn't hear a thing. I must've been dead to the world.

We ordered food, and Ledford and Tania started talking. Every time I added something, they looked at me like I was interrupting a private conversation, so I gave up. Ledford launched into his geocaching plans, and I nearly fell asleep in my French toast.

Ledford was talking about running around in the woods as a kid with his brothers and how they used to leave each other signs to follow so they wouldn't get lost. They would scratch a turtle into the dirt or draw one on a tree. Then he went into when they discovered geocaching.

"That sounds so fun," Tania said. She had to be lying. Tania wasn't an outdoors person. "So geocaches can look like anything?" she asked.

"Yes." Ledford dug in his pocket and pulled out something that looked like a screw. "Looks like a screw, right?"

We both nodded. He twisted off the top and pulled out a tiny rolled-up paper. "It's a geocache. People follow clues, find it, sign it, and hide it again."

He set it down and produced a fake spider. "Same with this—little compartment on the bottom."

"Wow," Tania said. "That's clever."

"I'm going to hide them all tomorrow on my day off. Anyone's welcome to help me."

Tania turned to me. "We should help, Ivy."

I swallowed my French toast and tried not to cringe. Running around the woods with Ledford and Tania sounded like a punishment for a crime. Especially if they were going to spend that time flirting. It was more than I wanted to sign on for.

"I have a lot to do with wedding plans and stuff," I said, thinking that should excuse me.

"Well, I'll come," Tania volunteered.

"Great," Ledford said. "I'll meet you out front tomorrow at eight."

He stood, and so did Tania. Her eyes narrowed as she looked down at me.

"Something wrong?" Ledford asked.

"You look taller sitting down," Tania said.

I rolled my eyes. What was wrong with these two? Maybe they were a match made in heaven—neither one knew how to keep their opinions to themselves.

"I'm probably taller than you without the heels," Ledford said.

"Maybe."

"So tomorrow," I said, changing the subject. "Sounds like a lot of fun."

Ledford nodded and excused himself.

I turned to Tania. "I can't believe you just insulted him."

"He's short! Why didn't you warn me? Now I have to avoid him."

"Except you can't—you agreed to go hide caches tomorrow."

She groaned. "I'll think of an excuse."

"You will not. You can't judge people on their height."

"I can. Short is fine for some people, but I need a tall man. Makes me feel more feminine."

"Are you kidding me right now?"

"No."

"He's totally ripped, though."

"Yeah, I noticed. Short guys work out to compensate. It's sad, really."

"Oh my heck, you are so superficial."

"I just know what I want. You want me to change my values for a guy?"

"That is not a value. That's a judgmental opinion."

"Whatever."

"You're still going tomorrow."

"Fine, but then I'm moving on."

"Ivy!" Boyd said, stepping into the diner. "I heard about the dead man." He slid into Ledford's empty seat. "Hey, Tania. Weird to see you back."

She crossed her arms and muttered something.

He grinned. "What was that?"

Boyd's taken on a grandfatherly role with me. If I solve a mystery, Boyd's usually right there beside me. He might not be any more subtle than Tania, though.

Boyd turned to Tania. "How was the slammer?"

She arched a brow. "Seriously?"

He chuckled and rubbed his goatee. "Alright, tell me about the dead guy."

"Jett thinks he was hit in the head. His name was Elias Prescott."

"And there was cake all over him?"

"Yeah."

"Jett didn't get home until early this morning."

I glanced at Tania. "Boyd and Jett are roommates."

"And after the wedding?" she asked. "Boyd moving in, too?"

"I'm moving into one of the new condos in town. Should be finished any time now."

"I can't believe how much has changed." Tania gazed out the window. "I wasn't gone that long, and the town looks different."

"The condos are changing things," I agreed.

"And I'm the mayor now," Boyd said. "Anyone tell you that?"

Tania's eyes went wide. "The mayor? Like, people voted you in?"

"Yep. And it probably had nothing to do with the fact that no one was running against me."

"Ah. Got it."

Boyd stood. "I'm going up to check on Creepers. He probably misses me."

"He checks on your cat?"

"Yeah. They're friends. You alright?"

"Fine," she said. "It just seems like you barreled into town and took over. It's hard to wrap my head around."

I bit back a retort. It probably did feel that way since I ran the diner she'd grown up in and was marrying the guy she'd crushed on. I couldn't exactly expect her to be thrilled about that. I wasn't going to feel guilty, though. She'd made her choices.

Chapter 5

I stood in front of Jett's desk, eyeing the piles of folders stacked so precariously I half expected them to avalanche onto the floor. His mug was tipped to the side, a dark ring left on the paperwork beneath it. Typical Jett—half order, half chaos.

"So you don't think Ledford and Tania are going to pick out wedding colors anytime soon?" Jett asked, folding his arms.

"Not a chance," I said. "And it's too bad because they were getting along."

He flipped through a file without really looking at it. "I thought you wanted Ledford to fall for Jane."

"Shhh!" I darted a look over my shoulder. Jane, the sheriff's secretary, was at her desk, typing furiously. Her expression was bland, but her ears were practically perked like a cat's. I shut the door. "I did, but she's made it clear it's never going to happen."

His eyes lit up. "So I win."

I scowled. "Yes."

We'd made a bet about Ledford and Jane, and now I was stuck cleaning up after Creepers and Jett's dog, Conan, for a year. I loved Conan, but I was secretly hoping Boyd would keep him for most of that year.

"I won't really make you do it all." Jett tapped his pen against the desk. "I just like to tease you."

"Tania's so set in her ways. Ledford's probably the same height as her."

"Yeah, well, I know she's your cousin, but I wouldn't wish her on my worst enemy."

"That's what I was thinking the other day. I just hope she's nice tomorrow when they hide the caches."

"You should go with them."

"I already claimed wedding plans."

"I think we have everything ready."

"Maybe, but do you really want me stuck out there with those two?"

"It might make a good story someday."

I let out a breath, tracing a finger along the edge of his desk. "I guess. I might go. But if I hide them, I can't help find them."

"Ledford's been hiding them for months. There'll still be some you don't know about."

"I'll think about it."

The door opened, and Jane poked her head in. "Sheriff Malone? There's someone here to see you."

"Thanks, Jane."

I left the building and went back to the diner. I hadn't made cookies in a while, and José was probably sick of doing it. Not that he'd ever complain. He was the reason Sue's Diner ran as smoothly as it did, and I couldn't ask for a better manager.

I still wondered about the dead guy. I'd meant to ask Jett, but I'd gotten sidetracked telling him about Ledford and Tania.

José was flipping burgers, and Anton was stirring something on the stove. We only needed two cooks on Tuesdays—any more and people started looking for things to do.

"I thought you'd be out sniffing for the killer." Anton glanced over his shoulder.

"There might not be a killer," I said. "He could've broken in and hit his head on the pan or something."

"Because that makes total sense."

I grabbed a rag from the counter and tossed it at him. "Aren't you the one always telling me to stay out of this stuff?"

He grinned. "Yeah, but I've learned you don't listen."

"I'm going to try. I don't want to ruin my wedding by chasing another case."

"Good call," José said. "I bet Jett appreciates you letting him do his job."

"I hope so, because it isn't easy."

I plugged in the mixer and started gathering ingredients. Our wedding was so close, but it felt like it was taking forever to get here.

*

I stood outside the diner with Tania and Ledford the next day, wondering how I'd let her talk me into this. Judging from the way Ledford hadn't spoken to her since we arrived, he'd heard the height comment loud and clear.

Tania had spent yesterday getting her nails and eyelashes done, and today, she'd shown up in an outfit that didn't fit this outing in any way—a pink tank top and shorts I'd love to donate at least three more inches of fabric to.

"I have my backpack full of geocaches," Ledford said. "It might take the better part of the day, so let's get going."

It was always weird seeing Ledford in regular clothes—jeans, a button-up, and sunglasses.

"You might want better shoes," he said, eyeing Tania's wedge sandals.

"There's nothing you can do in hiking boots that I can't do in these." She held her foot out to show off the shoe.

Ledford shrugged, trying to look like he hadn't been looking at her leg. "You know you have to get yourself out of the woods as well as in, right? No one's carrying you."

She glared. "I'll be in better shape than you by the end."

I wasn't overly thrilled to be with these two.

"We'll see," he said. "Let's go."

I tightened my blond ponytail, and the three of us climbed into Ledford's car. We drove about ten miles to a heavily wooded area. He wanted to start with the farthest caches and work our way back toward town.

We got out, and I looked around. The morning air was cool, and birds were chattering in the trees.

"The key to geocaching," Ledford explained, "is finding the perfect spot and leaving the perfect clue. You want a mix—some easier, some harder. People like different skill levels."

"Do you play Dungeons and Dragons too?" Tania asked.

Ledford frowned. "What does that have to do with anything?"

She fiddled with her mood ring. "Just trying to figure you out." Then she leaned close to me and whispered, "He's the guy I would've made fun of in high school."

Ledford's eyes narrowed, and I hoped we'd make it through without anyone actually getting killed.

"Let's go this way," he said. "There's a stream and a few good places to hide things."

We walked until we could hear water. When we reached the small stream, we stopped.

"I want to show you what a geocache is like," Ledford said, looking at me and ignoring Tania. He pulled up his phone. "I have the app. So there is a clue here that says, 'Near a red rock, don't get wet.'"

"And that's possible to find?" Tania asked. "The stream is long."

"Yes, but we also have coordinates, so we know it's really close. Why don't you two look for it so you get a feel for what we're doing? Or Tania can look for that one, and Ivy can look for the one that says 'Near the base of the biggest tree.' Then you won't mess each other up."

Tania wrinkled her nose and stepped near the water. "I'm not getting wet."

I looked around and found the biggest tree in the area. I walked over and pushed through the weeds. I hoped the chiggers weren't out today. I did not want to get bug bites right before my wedding.

I saw a box hidden in the brush and pulled it out, shaking off whatever creepy things might have found it first.

"Found it!" I called.

Tania looked up from the stream. "Already?"

"Great," Ledford said. "Open it and write your name on the log. You can take something out if there's anything in there, but if you do, you need to put something else in return."

I pried the metal box open and looked in to see a bunch of jewelry. "There's no paper."

"Then just take something."

I wasn't going to go through a bunch of junk jewelry, so I closed it and hid it again.

"I think I found mine," Tania said, pulling up a small plastic tube. I walked over, and she pulled out a rolled-up paper and a pencil. She wrote her name under the other names and returned it to its place under a red rock. "Too easy."

"Those were both supposed to be easy," Ledford said, taking out his spider cache. "These are the hard types. I'm going to put it on a tree."

"How original," Tania said. "A spider on a tree."

"That's what makes it hard," he said. "People aren't going to find it without work because it looks normal."

"If that makes you feel creative."

"How did you get out of jail? Annoyed the guards, and they couldn't take you anymore?"

She crossed her arms. "What do you know about anything? Shouldn't you be out trying to solve a murder?"

"I'm not on duty today." He pursed his lips and took his fake spider over to the tree.

"Climb and put it up higher," I said.

"I'm not in a tree-climbing mood," he grumbled.

"I'll do it."

He handed it to me, and I started climbing, glad for my sensible shoes and not Tania's.

"While you're doing that, I'll have Tania take this one over that way. Find us when you're done."

"Alright." I climbed higher, but not too high. I doubted most people wanted to find themselves at the top of a tree. I put the spider in a place just high enough and still in sight of anyone who climbed up a little.

I got back down and brushed off my jeans. Finding these would be fun. I hoped Ledford had a bunch I didn't know about, so it would be a challenge. I took a few steps and stopped to dump a rock from my shoe.

When I finished, I walked in the direction he'd indicated. There were no signs of them. The trees here were dense, and the breeze made me wish I had a jacket. It was quieter than it should have been—no voices and no twigs snapping underfoot, just the faint rush of the stream behind me.

"Ledford!" I called. My voice seemed to drop into the woods and vanish. I tried again, louder. Still nothing.

I called both of their phones. No answer. The only sound was a distant rustle, like something moving in the underbrush, but when I turned, nothing was there. If it were anyone else, I would think they were messing with me, but there was no way they would prank me together.

Five minutes stretched to thirty. My heart kicked harder with each one. I tried calling Jett, but the call went to voicemail.

"Tania!" I yelled. "This isn't funny!"

I called Boyd.

"Hey, Ivy."

"Boyd? I'm out in the woods somewhere, and I lost Ledford and Tania. It's been thirty minutes, and I don't know where they could be. They aren't answering their phones, and neither is Jett."

"Stay calm. I'll find Jett, and we'll come."

"How will you find me? I don't even know where I am. I can't even find the car."

"Use your phone's GPS and ask where you are."

"Right."

"Don't panic. We'll be there soon."

I asked my phone how to get out of here, and it showed me the area I was in. I still took a few wrong turns because the location wasn't exact, but I eventually made my way through the trees and came to Ledford's car. Jett could track my phone, so he should be able to find the place.

I sat on the hood of the car and ignored all the bugs buzzing in my face. If they didn't hurry, I would go into full panic mode. Ledford and Tania wouldn't sneak off together, so they must be lost.

This could be really bad. Tania didn't know how to do anything, and Ledford wasn't going to be sympathetic to her and her silly shoes.

After what felt like forever, Jett's truck pulled into view. I got off the hood and waited. Jett and Boyd climbed out of the truck and came over.

I tried to smile, but I'd had too long to let my imagination take over. "I still can't find them," I said with a shaky voice. "What if they got mauled by a bear or something?"

Jett pulled me into a hug. "Not likely. There aren't a lot of bears around here."

"Then what? They weren't going far, and they disappeared so fast. I yelled, and I looked around. Something's wrong."

"It's easy to get lost in a place like this."

"They didn't have enough time to get far enough not to hear me yell."

Boyd peered into the trees. "Maybe they lost you on purpose. Wanted some alone time." He wagged his eyebrows, and I cringed.

"No way. They've been at each other's throats all morning."

My phone pinged, and I looked down. "Tania sent me a text. 'Sorry I missed your call. What did you need?'" I glared at the phone. "What do I need? Seriously?"

Me: Where are you? I've been looking all over.

Tania: Sorry. We wandered too far.

Me: Where are you now? I'm at the car. Jett and Boyd came because I freaked out.

Tania: Don't worry. Go home with them. We'll finish up here.

"She said we should go. They went too far." I kicked at the ground. "I feel funny about this. I'm going to call her."

The phone rang four times, then she answered.

"What, Ivy?"

"Is everything alright?"

"Yes."

"Are you lying?"

She snorted. "Why would I be lying?"

"I just find it really weird that you would wander off with Ledford."

"I can do what I want."

I frowned. "I'm not saying... You know what? Never mind. I'll see you at home." I hung up and put my phone away. "I don't know what they're doing, but they seem to be fine."

"Great," Jett said. "Let's go."

We got into the truck, and Boyd patted my shoulder. "Don't worry. They're fine. Probably out making the most of being alone."

"I told you, they don't even like each other."

"Things change."

"Not that fast."

"You never got along with Tania, and it's no secret you and Ledford aren't besties. I'm surprised you're so upset."

I glared. "You know me, Boyd. I'd be worried no matter who was lost out there."

"Right. You have been known to help people who aren't your favorite."

"It's one thing that makes Ivy amazing," Jett said. "She's going to do what's right, and she cares."

"True," Boyd said. "But it's also what always gets her in trouble."

Chapter 6

"What if they're dead?" I asked, pacing Jett's office. My shoes still had dried mud, and it was flaking onto the floor as I went. The office rarely got dirty, so I figured I was just helping keep the janitor in their job.

He glanced up from his computer. "They aren't dead. You talked to Tania."

"That was hours ago. And now, both of their phones are going to voicemail."

"Cell service is spotty in some places."

"Not there. It's close enough to town."

"Don't jump to the worst-case scenario. I bet Tania just got the geocaching bug and they're having a great time."

I took a deep breath and let it out. "Well, I bet one of them killed the other one, and whoever is left is running across Kansas heading straight for Mexico."

Jett's mouth twitched. "Do you hear yourself, sweetheart?"

"You need to do something."

"Ivs, I'm trying to solve an actual murder here. I can't take off and go chasing nothing."

I knew he was probably right, but this was weird. If it were Tania and any of the other deputies, I wouldn't think anything about it. It also bothered me that two of the people I only barely tolerate had gone missing when they were with me. Would that make me a suspect?

Sure, Ledford and I had put aside our differences, but people would remember when we used to fight every time we were near each other. And Tania? We weren't cozy even before she went to prison.

"They might be fine, but you should have been there. The woods were so quiet and eerie. I didn't give them a chance to get far. When I yelled, they had to have heard me."

"You're looping, Ivs."

"I know."

"Come here."

I walked around his desk, feeling like a toddler seeking reassurance from a parent. He pulled me down onto his lap and clasped his hands at my stomach. I rested the back of my head on his shoulder, and he pressed his cheek to mine.

"Ledford is highly skilled. He's one of those people who could survive in the woods with nothing but a pair of fingernail clippers and a rock. They're going to be fine." He kissed my cheek. "Alright?"

I nodded. He was right. Probably. And I was distracting him from what he needed to be doing.

There was a knock, then the door opened, and Deputy Hayes poked his head in. He cleared his throat, and I felt the temperature in my face go up ten degrees, but Jett didn't let me go.

"Hayes," Jett said. "Would you mind taking a break from paperwork and going out to the last spot Ledford was seen? Ivy can tell you where that was."

Hayes ran a hand over his brown curls. "Anything to get out of paperwork. Is something wrong with Ledford?"

"I don't think so, but Ivy's worried. Ledford and Ivy's cousin, Tania, are out in the woods, and they haven't answered their phones in a while."

"Okay. So we're just making sure they didn't fall in the creek or get eaten by a snake or something?"

Jett chuckled, and I glared. He was going to be sorry if that had happened.

"Pretty much."

I wiggled out of Jett's arms and stood. "Take me with you. I can show you where Ledford parked."

"I'm not sure that's a good idea," Hayes said.

Jett gave him a sympathetic smile. "If you don't take her, she'll stow away in your trunk or something."

I shot him a look.

He grinned. "You know it's true."

"I would not. I'd follow in my own car."

Hayes looked at Jett, who shrugged.

"I'll take my own car and Boyd," I said. "You can follow us."

Hayes looked like he wanted to argue, but then thought better of it.

I hurried to the diner and found Boyd in the kitchen talking to José. I grabbed him, and we got in my car. Deputy Hayes was in his patrol car behind us.

"I think we're wasting time," Boyd said as we drove.

"I hope so, but I'm nervous. If it were Tania and anyone else, I wouldn't think twice. They didn't say a nice thing to each other all morning."

"It only takes a minute to change your mind about someone."

"Not Tania."

"Ledford grew on you."

"After months."

"Well, I have nothing better to do than look for people who aren't lost." He rubbed his bald head. "Not sure how ready I am to trample through the woods, though."

"That's what you say, but I know you, Boyd. If I look the other way, you'll be stuck in a tree or falling in the stream."

He laughed. "You know that's right. I should work on not getting myself into those kinds of fixes."

I looked ahead and frowned. "I could have sworn Ledford's car was parked just up there."

"Then they left."

"I guess so. I should have checked in my apartment to see if Tania was back before we came."

I pulled over, and Hayes followed suit. I stepped out, scanning the empty stretch of gravel. This had to be the spot. The tire marks were fresh, but the woods on either side were still and quiet in a way that felt wrong.

Hayes and Boyd got out and looked around.

"Ledford was parked right here," I told him.

"So there's no problem?" Hayes asked, looking everywhere but at me.

"I guess."

"Don't wander around this area alone. In fact, avoid this place if you can. It's not... the best place to hang out."

"Okay?" I said, hoping he'd say more. He didn't.

"Then if you don't need me, I'll head back."

I didn't have an argument for that.

His gaze went to the trees for another second, then he climbed into his car and drove off.

Boyd watched him leave. "He was acting weird. He's usually a little more friendly."

"He wasn't unfriendly."

"Yeah, but did you see the way his eyes were darting around?"

I wrinkled my nose. "It might be because he walked in when Jett and I were... doing nothing, but I think it made him feel awkward."

Boyd chuckled. "Doing nothing?"

"Nothing worth getting embarrassed about."

"I've witnessed some of those moments."

"You wouldn't if you knocked."

He laughed again. "Knocking takes some of the fun out of life—and the surprises don't hit as hard."

I shook my head and smiled. "Get in the car. I'm not taking this from you."

I tried calling Tania again before getting in. Still voicemail. I slid behind the wheel and started driving.

"Try Ledford," I muttered as the trees blurred past.

"Stop the car," Boyd said sharply.

I pulled over and followed his gaze. A car sat half-hidden in the trees.

He pointed. "That's Hayes."

I squinted. "Why would he pull over here?"

"Maybe he saw something."

"Or he's up to something."

I eased the car to the opposite shoulder and pulled up a little, then cut the engine. "Why would he pull over here?"

Boyd shrugged. "Maybe he saw something."

"Or... he's behind something," I muttered. "Let's go."

"Where?"

"To see what Hayes is doing."

Boyd unbuckled with a sigh. "Alright, but you know Hayes isn't Jett, right? He might not take kindly to being followed."

"It's fine. I think he's scared of me."

He chuckled. "Scared of you? Probably. You are a bit of a loose cannon."

We got out and walked to where we'd seen the car. Hayes was pulling something from his trunk and put it in his pocket. He touched the gun at his side and glanced around.

"Move over before he sees us," I muttered, pulling Boyd behind a large sycamore. "He's not innocent. It doesn't make sense for him to stop here. I mean, what's he doing?"

"Maybe his job? I mean, everyone knows Ivy Clark is going to butt into things. He must want to look around without us, just to make sure everything's alright."

"But why here? He put himself farther from where I told him the car had been."

"Who knows?"

Hayes slammed the trunk and went deeper into the woods, not looking back.

I hurried forward, slipping from tree to tree, assuming Boyd would follow. I didn't care what he thought—something was going on. Hayes moved fast, forcing me into a ridiculous game of arboreal leapfrog that I was sure Boyd would mock later.

Hayes stopped. So did I. He touched the trunk of a tall oak, glanced up, then scanned the woods before starting to climb.

My eyes narrowed. Boyd caught up, puffing.

"What's he doing?" he asked between breaths.

"Climbing a tree?"

"And you were worried I'd do that."

"I bet he can get himself down."

"Get stuck in one tree and you never hear the end of it."

I smiled at the memory, then watched Hayes settle on a branch and reach for something tucked against the trunk. A small box. He opened it, frowned, then shut it and slid it back into place.

He dropped to the ground in a crouch.

"Wow," I muttered. It was an impressive landing.

Boyd poked my shoulder. "Should Jett be worried?"

I shot him a glare. "Not at all."

Hayes got down on his knees and rummaged through the weeds, mumbling to himself. He stood, brushed off his pants, and started deeper into the trees.

"Dang it." I turned to Boyd. "Do we check the tree or follow him? He knew exactly where that was."

"Don't know. I just come for the thrill."

I needed to decide fast.

"Follow him." I couldn't lose him—especially if he knew anything about Ledford and Tania.

"I'll stay by the tree," Boyd said. "I can't move that fast."

"Don't climb it."

"Alright."

I trailed Hayes for ten minutes, ducking behind trees, careful not to snap a twig. Then—he was gone. My pulse spiked. He'd been right in front of me. The creek gurgled past the last tree where I'd seen him, and I darted forward, figuring he'd kept straight.

Arms yanked me back.

I shrieked and drove my elbow into solid muscle. Hayes grunted but locked me tighter, pinning my arms.

"What are you doing, Miss Clark? I could've hurt you."

"What do you mean, *could have*?" I twisted, stomping down hard on his foot. He barely flinched but loosened enough for me to rip free—sending us both tumbling straight into the creek.

Cold water punched the air from my lungs. I shoved Hayes off and sat upright, completely soaked and shivering.

Hayes stood dripping, hair plastered to his forehead, his usual calm eyes flaring with something sharp. He held out a hand. "Why are you following me?"

I crossed my arms, partly from defiance and partly to keep my teeth from chattering. "Why are *you* out here?" I stood without his help.

"I don't have to explain myself to you."

I stomped toward the bank but slipped on the mud. Hayes caught my arm, and the momentum yanked us both onto the shore in a graceless heap. My palms slid out from under me, elbows hitting hard.

By the time I pushed upright, Hayes was already standing, mud streaked down his shirt, smirking. "I didn't believe the stories I'd heard about you. Now I do."

He held out his hand again, like I might suddenly be grateful. Not a chance.

I got to my feet and cringed. I was completely soaked and covered in mud. Cold mud. Spring wasn't as warm as I might have liked.

I gave him one last sharp glare and started back to find Boyd.

"You aren't going to tell me why you're following me?"

I glanced over my shoulder. "Not unless you're going to tell me what you're doing out here."

He pursed his lips.

"That's what I thought."

Chapter 7

I walked through the woods, dripping everywhere. My jeans clung to my legs like cold seaweed. I could hear Hayes slogging along behind me, and I wanted to tell him to go away—but where would he go?

I reminded myself I'd liked him just fine until today. One bizarre run-in shouldn't change that. Still, there was no way he was innocent here.

Footsteps pounded toward us, and Jett burst around a cluster of trees, skidding to a stop. His gaze swept over me, then landed on Hayes.

I kept moving toward him.

"What...? Why are you both covered in mud?"

I glanced back at Hayes and scowled.

"She was following me," Hayes said, sounding a little too nervous. "I didn't know who she was, so I grabbed her, and she threw us in the creek."

Jett blinked. "I don't know why I'm ever surprised." He grinned. "You look good in mud."

I stepped right into him, wrapping my muddy arms around his clean shirt. "So do you."

"I'm going to go," Hayes said.

Jett nodded.

I released him. "Don't let him go. He's a suspect."

"A suspect in what?" Hayes asked, arching a brow.

"Uh... being out in the woods doing something."

Hayes blinked. "Airtight case you've got there."

"Ivs," Jett said, "I love you, but I think your detective skills just hit rock bottom."

"He wasn't even worried about Ledford and Tania, then he came out here snooping around."

Jett tipped his head toward Hayes. Hayes gave a quick nod and headed to his car without a word.

"Hayes is working on something. It makes sense he'd be looking around here."

"Why?"

He leaned closer and whispered, "None of your business, snoopy."

I crossed my gross arms. "I'll take your word this time, but only because I'm cold and I want a hot shower."

"You're freezing."

"Tell me something I don't know."

"Ledford's car is at the diner. I didn't go in because Boyd called me."

"Oh good," I said, leaning into him. He wrapped his arms around my soggy, muddy self. "I've been worried."

"Come on. Let's get you to your car."

We met Boyd at my car. He was already sitting inside. Jett went to his truck and came back with a towel and something black. He draped the towel over my seat and handed me a jacket.

I pulled it on and slid into place.

"I'll see you back in town," Jett said.

I nodded, and he closed the door.

"Wow," Boyd said. "You're as muddy as Hayes. He didn't look happy."

"He knew he was being followed. I don't want to talk about it."

He chuckled. "Alright, but I want to hear it eventually."

We drove in silence. I was grateful for the jacket—it was colder than I'd realized.

I dropped Boyd off, then headed to the diner. Ledford's car was still there. Good. I wasn't going to hunt him down, though. I needed a shower.

Around back, I climbed the stairs to my place. Creepers meowed when I came in, then hopped onto the couch like he was claiming it.

After my shower, I sank down beside him. "You missed all the excitement."

He yawned.

"How are you always tired? You sleep all the time."

He gave me a slow blink, as if to say, *What's your point?*

"I don't have a point. It's been a crazy day. Has Tania been up? Is she in the diner?"

Creepers hopped off the couch and padded away. Figured.

I sighed and pulled on a clean pair of shoes, then went down to the dining area.

We had a few patrons in our booths. I smiled at them all as I passed. No Ledford or Tania.

"Miss Clark?"

I turned to a booth to see a woman, about thirty-five, with black hair and dark eyes. She looked familiar, but I couldn't place her.

"Yes?" I asked.

"I'm Danica Whitaker. I'm not sure we've met."

I shook her hand. "Nice to meet you."

She gave me a small, uneasy smile. "I might have offended Tania a few minutes ago. Will you tell her I didn't mean anything by my comment?"

"Of course. She was here?"

"Yes." Danica hesitated, and her gaze jumped to the window.

"Do you know where she went?"

Her brows came together as if she were thinking. "Umm... she left with one of the deputies. I wasn't paying a lot of attention to which one."

It had to be Ledford. I glanced out the window. Ledford's car was still there. They must have walked.

"Thanks," I said. "I hope you're enjoying your food."

"I am, thanks."

I went into the kitchen to see Anton, José, and Carrie all working on different things.

"Did anyone talk to Ledford or Tania this afternoon?" I asked.

José turned from the stove. "Nope. Haven't looked out. Ask Livy."

"She was talking to customers."

"Lose them?" Carrie asked.

I shrugged. "It's weird. Those two were sniping at each other all morning, and now they're off together, ignoring their phones."

José laughed. "I'd never put the two of them together. Tania's too stuck-up for him."

"That's for sure," Anton agreed.

Livy came in and stuck an order on the bulletin board. A stray strand of red hair had come loose from her ponytail and hung in her face.

"Livy?" I asked. "Have you seen Ledford and Tania?"

"No. They haven't been in—at least not to eat."

"Has it been busy today?"

"Not bad. Pretty normal for a Wednesday." She grabbed a rag, got it wet, and headed back out, probably to wipe down a table.

"You guys need help?"

"Nope." Carrie shook her head. "Go get all your wedding planning in."

"I think we've done just about everything."

No one said anything. I was killing the vibe in the kitchen, but I had nowhere to go. I grabbed a small plate and a piece of cheesecake, then I went out to the dining area and sat at an empty booth.

Oliver Radcliffe came in, and Livy rushed over, then showed him to a booth.

"Hi, Oliver," Danica said as he passed her.

He turned and gave her a killer smile. "Hey, Danica. Long time."

"You want to sit with me?"

He shrugged. "Sure." He sat across from her and gave Livy his order. I didn't know Oliver well. I was almost sure he worked at the new auto body shop. The one where the dead guy, Elias Prescott, worked. If he weren't with Danica, I would try to start a conversation. I thought about the van in the city delivering the package. Same shop.

Danica's smile was huge. I could only see the back of Oliver's dark hair from my position. Danica had a crush. I'd bet Oliver was at least ten years older than she was, but who was I to judge?

"What happened to your face?" Danica asked. There wasn't a lot of privacy in this place.

His hand went up to his cheek. I wished I could see. Jett was right to call me snoopy. "A piece of wire flipped up and cut me. I'd like to say I've never done that before, but that would be a lie." He chuckled. "You need to pay attention when you work with cars, but I get in the zone."

They talked about boring things until I lost interest. I ate my cheesecake and stared blankly out the window. When I finally got out of my thoughts, Ledford's car was gone. Great. I'd missed them, and I'd even been looking out the window. Maybe Jett was right, and my detective skills were getting rusty. Not that I had any real skills. I was just nosy enough to figure some things out.

It wasn't like I really needed to talk to them. Danica had seen them, and they obviously had driven here.

I went back upstairs to Creepers. Boyd was in my apartment playing with Conan.

"Hey," I said, sitting on the recliner. "Are you going to take Conan to your place when you move?" The dog was technically Jett's, but Boyd spent the most time with him. I worried about having a dog over the diner.

"It's up to Jett. I wouldn't mind keeping him with me. I can't clean up after him, so Jett would have to come do that."

Conan ran over and jumped up against my leg. I picked up the little ball of white fluff and put him on my lap. He curled up, and I rubbed his back. We talked until Boyd got tired and left. I'd had trouble keeping up my part of the conversation. My mind was jumping between wedding thoughts and Tania.

There was a knock, and then Jett came in. His hair was messier than usual, and he yawned.

"Long day?" I asked.

"So long." He dropped onto the couch and patted the spot next to him.

"You want me to stand? You seem to forget I had a physical fight with one of your deputies today. I haven't moved in an hour."

He smiled and stood, pulling me to my feet, and flopped us both down on the couch. He wrapped his arms around me and sighed. "You're lucky Hayes didn't arrest you for assaulting an officer."

"What? He assaulted me."

"That's not the way Hayes tells it."

"Oh yeah?"

"He's a great storyteller. He had everyone in the office rolling in their seats."

"Great. Now I have to be embarrassed every time I go into your office."

"No. Everyone already knows what you're like. People appreciate it."

"So I'm the town joke?"

"Nah. That would be Boyd, but he owns it."

"I don't want to think about today. It's been a mess."

"We can end it better than it started." He kissed my cheek, and I melted.

I let myself lean into him and met his lips, but my mind wasn't ready to let go of the day yet. Somewhere out there, Hayes was climbing trees and digging through weeds — and I still had no idea why.

Chapter 8

I woke up to another crash in the diner. I sat up in my bed and listened. Tania, maybe? Right before I'd fallen asleep, I'd gotten a text from her telling me she'd found another place to stay. I'd texted back, and she hadn't answered.

I got out of bed and opened the door that went downstairs. Everything was dark. I moved carefully down the steps, my bare feet not making a sound. I hated the fact that crashes in the kitchen were becoming a common occurrence.

Peeking into the diner showed me a dark room, just the shadowy outlines of booths. I tiptoed through and over near the kitchen. No light came from under the door. My heart thudded as I pushed it open.

Moonlight spilled through the window, catching a tall figure at the island. His back was toward me.

I scanned the shadows for a weapon but saw nothing. On my toes, I crept closer—and before he knew I was there, I jumped on his back.

"Mmmfff!" he said.

My arms tightened over his shoulders, and I had no idea what my next move should be. Biting was a sucker move, but maybe my only option. I put my mouth close to his neck—then froze. Something about this felt too familiar.

"Ivs, if you bite me, I swear—"

"Jett? Oh, thank goodness." I slid to my feet, and he turned to face me. "For a second, I thought you were a burglar."

"For a second? And you body-slammed me before con-firming that?"

"Well, what the heck are you doing here? What am I supposed to think?"

"Someone called about a suspicious person wandering around the square. Turned out to be nothing, so..." He shrugged. "I figured I'd grab a cookie."

"In the middle of the night? Do I have to take away your diner key? You almost gave me a heart attack."

"Sorry. I thought you were going to go full vampire on me and bite me."

"I was. Hard."

"Well, I guess I escaped a rabies shot."

"I don't have rabies."

He laughed and pulled me against him. I leaned into his chest with a sigh. "You owe me. I was sound asleep."

"Did Tania come back?"

"No. She texted. She found somewhere else to stay."

"Where?"

"No clue." I tilted my head up. "I'm tired. Kiss me good, then get out of here."

"I would like nothing better." He kissed me, and I remembered all the reasons I loved him.

"I wish every midnight check-up ended like this," he murmured.

"I wish you'd stop talking."

He chuckled and kissed me again.

Someone jiggled the back doorknob, and we broke apart, freezing. I looked up at Jett but couldn't read his expression in the dark.

"Shhh," he whispered. "Stay here."

He moved toward the door, my heartbeat thudding faster with each quiet step. Through the shadows, I saw him draw his gun.

I bit my lip, praying he'd be safe.

Jett flung the door open—

Deputy Hayes stood there.

"Hayes?" Jett said. "What are you doing here?"

Hayes put a hand to his chest. "Having heart failure, it feels like."

"I hope you have a good reason for being here."

"I got a call—someone said a man was sneaking around the diner."

I smiled to myself. Apparently, Jett wasn't as stealthy as he thought.

"It was me, and I wasn't sneaking."

"Liar," I said.

Hayes jumped. "Anyone else hiding in the dark?"

"No, just me. And you were sneaking, Jett. That's why I almost decapitated you."

"Decapitated? With your teeth?"

Hayes shuddered. "Not sure I want to know this story. I'll see you later."

Jett closed the door.

"Why would he try the knob?" I asked. "Screams suspicious to me."

"Hayes is on the level. I trust him."

"Says the guy who steals cookies in the middle of the night."

"Hey. We're almost married—half the cookies are mine by default. You're sharing, right?"

I laughed. "Not if you wake me up in the middle of the night."

"I'm staying on your couch."

"Why?"

"Just in case."

"In case what?"

"I trust Hayes," he said, glancing at the door, "but I don't like that he tried the knob."

"Ever since I moved to Muddy Creek, my life's been nothing but chills and a racing heartbeat."

"I hope I'm responsible for the heartbeat — in a good way."

I smiled. "Oh, you are."

⚘

The following morning, I texted Tania while mixing pancakes and cooking them. Carrie wasn't feeling well, and Anton had a quick dental emergency, so we were short-staffed. I couldn't figure out why I was so uneasy about Tania and Ledford. It wasn't like I had cuddly feelings for either of them, so worrying they might have both gone crazy shouldn't be on my mind.

Tania texted back. *Hey Ivie. I'm busy. Can we talk later? – ToniaH.*

My heart stopped. "José, sorry to ditch you. I'll be back." I didn't wait for a reply before I ran the few blocks to Jett's office. I busted in the front door and went straight into his office without knocking. He was talking to Hayes. They both looked at me.

"Something's wrong." I handed Jett my phone so he could read the text.

"What?"

"Both of our names are spelled wrong, and Tania never signs her name after a text. And even her last initial? That doesn't make sense."

"Tania never makes sense," Jett said.

I grabbed the phone and texted her back. *Where did you put my sweater?* I was grasping.

"Where's Ledford?" I asked.

"He called in sick."

"And you two don't see the problem with this?"

"I see a problem. He's probably lying and with Tania."

My phone pinged. *Did you look on my bed? – TaniaE*

I showed it to Jett. "What do you say about this? She didn't take my sweater. And now her last initial is an E?"

I swiped: *It's not there.*

"It does seem a little weird," Hayes said. "Ledford's a lot of things, but he's not a slacker."

"He's also never had a girlfriend," Jett reminded him.

Ping. *Try the couch - TaniaL.*

"She's going to spell HELP after her name," I said. "We have to do something!"

Jett frowned. "Send one more."

I typed: *Not there. Do you have it?*

I jiggled my leg. Maybe I didn't dislike Tania as much as I told myself. We had been close as kids. Sure, she wasn't that nice now, but those early memories were still alive.

Ping. *No. - TaniaP*

"Bam," I said. "She's in trouble."

Jett's jaw tightened. "Ask her if she's with Ledford."

You with Ledford?

Yes.

"Please tell me I'm not panicking alone," I said.

Jett shook his head. "I'm there with you."

"Danica said she saw them leave the diner together yesterday."

Hayes crossed his arms. "So she lied."

"Well, she said Tania and a deputy. She didn't know which one."

"Why lie?" Jett wondered. "What would she gain from that? Maybe they weren't in danger until later."

"Maybe she's in danger from Ledford," I said, not fully believing it.

"I'll swing by his place," Hayes said.

Jett nodded. "Call me as soon as you do. I'm going to make some calls."

Hayes left, and I wrung my hands. "What do I do?"

"Go back to the diner, and I'll let you know when we find them."

"You know I can't wait."

"We don't have any leads."

"I could go back to the woods."

"We know they were in town yesterday. That's why the car was back."

"Unless someone wants us to think that."

"Don't go to the woods."

"I left my pancakes cooking. I'd better hurry back and hope José noticed." I left quickly before he could make me promise anything.

I went into the diner and to the kitchen. José was flipping pancakes and stirring something with the other hand.

"Sorry," I said, hurrying over to the pancakes. "Tania's in trouble. Probably Ledford as well."

"What kind?"

"I don't know. She sent a cryptic text. Definitely asking for help, though."

"And you came to flip pancakes? That's out of character. I'd think you would be looking for her."

"I haven't decided what to do yet. I wonder if it's tied to the dead guy."

"How?"

"I don't know. I'm just trying to figure something out. I want to go back to the woods to see what Hayes was doing in the tree. Did I tell you about that?"

"Boyd did."

"Hayes is hiding something, but I don't know what. He tried to get into the diner last night. Danica might be involved as well. She told me she saw them, but if she did, it means they weren't in trouble until yesterday afternoon. I'm guessing whatever happened was in the morning. It makes more sense than Tania and Ledford running off together."

"Uh-huh."

"Are you listening to me?"

"Sort of. Sorry. I'm cooking three things."

I went on autopilot and helped José get the food out.

When the rush was over, I retold José everything that had happened. He looked at the texts and frowned.

"We should go see what Hayes was looking at in the tree."

"Now?" I asked.

"Yeah. What do you think? Slap a Closed sign on the door."

I nodded. If Tania and Ledford were in danger, losing the cost of part of the day wasn't important.

We served the people already in the diner, then José drove us to the place I hoped was the spot Hayes had been, and we went into the trees. Things around here all looked alike, but I'd studied the tree, and we were able to find it.

"I'll go up," José offered.

"No, I will. I'm... younger."

He raised his brow. "But are you in better shape?" José was a big runner, and I do Zumba. Judging by his arms, he did more than run.

"Maybe not, but I probably heal faster."

"Ha ha. Go on, then."

I climbed the tree to the spot I thought Hayes had been sitting and looked around. I felt around the trunk until my hand touched something metal. I grabbed the small rectangular box and climbed back down.

"What is it?" José asked, leaning forward.

"Let's see." I popped it open. More fake jewelry. "I think this is one of Ledford's geocaches. There was another one he showed us down a ways."

José picked up a gold necklace and frowned. "It looks real. I don't picture Ledford filling these things with decent-looking jewelry."

"He didn't seem to think anything about the first one I found." I thought for a minute. "Of course, he didn't see inside it. But if he placed it, he would know."

"Did he say he placed it?"

"No, he just told me the clue and said to find it."

"Why don't you go put it back. If Hayes is up to something, he'll probably know it was you if you take it."

"Why would someone hide jewelry in a tree?"

"No clue."

I climbed back up and replaced it, then we went over to the area I'd been in when I lost Ledford and Tania.

"I climbed that tree," I said, pointing, "and then when I got down, they were gone. Ledford said to find him that way, but they weren't there."

"Let's walk that way then," José said. "Watch the ground for any type of struggle."

"I feel like I would have heard if anything like that happened. I was fast. They couldn't have gotten far unless they were trying to ditch me."

We walked, and I scanned the ground and the trees. Nothing seemed out of the ordinary.

"What's this?" José said, picking something up off the ground.

I sucked in a breath as I looked at the fake screw. "That's one of Ledford's fake geocaches."

"He must have dropped it."

I felt my eyes light up. "Or he's sending us a message."

Chapter 9

"I doubt Ledford and Tania are out here," José said as he scanned the trees. "I mean, if they still have access to their phones, they could tell us if they were lost."

My brow furrowed. "But Tania's texts read like she was trying to appease someone. Like someone was reading her text, and she didn't want them to know she was asking for help."

"True, but if they were abducted, would someone really keep them out here? Since they left from this place, it would be the obvious spot for people to search."

"If we don't search here, I don't know what to do, and I have to do something."

José nodded. "I understand that. We can keep looking."

After an hour of not finding anything, we went back to the car. It felt like giving up, but we hadn't found anything since the screw geocache. I had it in my pocket. I pulled it out and unscrewed it. Inside was the small paper that Ledford put in so people could write their names on it. All that was on the paper was a little squiggly turtle.

José headed back to town, and I tried to remember something. Something about a turtle. It felt on the edge of my brain, but I wasn't sure why.

"What do we do now?" José asked.

"I don't have any ideas. I guess we have to wait until Jett finds something."

"If Carrie and Anton come in tomorrow, we can go search again if you want."

"What does Carrie have?"

"Don't know. Something's been bugging her on and off, but she won't go to the doctor. She's been nauseous and tired all the time. She gets back from the diner and goes right to bed."

I raised my brow and smiled at José's clueless gaze. "And it's been going on how long?"

"About three weeks. Today, she threw up, though. That's why she didn't come in."

"So... is it a nine-month sickness?"

José laughed. "No way. We're too old for that."

"Carrie's still in her early forties."

"Yeah, and people don't have babies when they reach that age."

"They actually do."

José swallowed and gripped the steering wheel. "No way. I'm old."

"Not that old."

"Too old for diapers."

I let it drop. José didn't talk again until we got to the diner. He kept drumming his fingers nervously against the wheel. He parked, and I climbed out of the car, then paused.

"The turtle," I said, showing the paper to José. "Ledford told Tania that he and his brothers used to draw turtles in the woods—on trees, in the dirt—so they wouldn't lose their way. I bet he drew this to tell us he's in trouble."

José took the paper, and his brows came together. "I'll open the diner back up. You go tell Jett."

Jett wasn't at the office when I got there. Standing on the sidewalk, I fought the urge to just pace in circles. Across the street, Levi's Auto Shop gleamed under the late-morning sun. If I couldn't find Jett, maybe I could at least learn something about the dead guy.

I entered the shop and rubbed my nose. The tang of oil and rubber hit me first, undercut by the faint hum of a radio in the back.

Oliver Radcliffe stood behind the counter, smiling. Tall, broad-shouldered, with dark hair and eyes that didn't seem to miss much, he had the kind of strength built from years of hauling engines instead of gym weights. A faint scent of motor oil hung in the air, and grease still smudged his fingers. On one hand, a shiny silver pinky ring caught the light—a little unexpected flash against all that grit.

I gave a tight smile. "Hello. How are you?"

"Good, good. What can I help you with?"

"I was wondering about Elias Prescott."

His smile slipped, the kind of fade you notice when someone's replaying a memory they wish they could forget. "That was quite a tragedy. We'll miss Elias around here."

"I didn't know him," I said. "I'm sorry for your loss. Were you close?"

He rested his elbows on the counter and leaned forward. "Not close like doing things after work together, but we had a friendly work relationship. He was a nice enough guy."

"Do you have any idea why he would have been in my diner?"

He shook his head. "No. Elias didn't seem like the breaking-and-entering type."

"Do you know if he had enemies?"

"Hmm. Not really. I mean, there's Levi, but he hates everyone. He treats everyone pretty much the same, so I doubt he would kill Elias over anyone else."

"And Levi owns this place?"

"Yeah."

"Is he here?"

"No. We don't have enough business to have more than one employee at a time, so we usually work alone. We do overlap a little, but not much. He'll be here tomorrow morning."

"Do you know where he lives?"

"No. I don't seek him out. He's my boss, not my friend. I shouldn't say it, but if I were going to take someone out, it would be Levi." He laughed when my eyebrows rose. "I'm kidding, but seriously, not my favorite person."

The door opened, and Danica came in. She smiled when she saw me. "Hi, Miss Clark. Hello, Oliver."

I nodded.

"Hey, Danica," Oliver said. "Only one delivery today." He handed her a box, his pinky ring catching the light again.

Her smile slipped a little.

Oliver gave her a sympathetic smile and tipped his head slightly in my direction, almost too subtly to notice. Danica nodded.

"I should be going," I said, not understanding what was happening, just that I was interrupting something. "Thanks." I turned and left, once again clueless on the sidewalk.

I glanced back through the glass doors—and my brows lifted. Danica was already around the counter, her lips all over Oliver. Ah. She'd just been worried my presence was ruining her make-out time.

Jett's truck pulled up to the station, so I hurried across the street. He climbed out, and I hugged him from behind.

"Whoa!" he said, turning. "Man, Ivs. You shouldn't sneak up on me like that. You know I have a gun."

"Sneak? I just ran like a bulldozer from across the street. You should have heard me."

He chuckled. "I didn't."

"What does Danica Whitaker do for a living?"

"She delivers packages or picks things up for people. No one wants to drive to the city, so she goes twice a week to pick up anything a person might need. You'd be surprised how many of us are too lazy to go get our own things."

"So you've hired her?"

"A few times."

"How many is a few?"

He flashed me his perfect Jett smile. "About once a week."

"I'd never met her until this week. I'm guessing she's dating Oliver at the auto body shop?"

"Nah, she's dating Levi."

My lips puckered as I thought.

Jett's eyes narrowed. "What's that face? It's new. You want me to kiss you, or is it the newest online trend?"

I swatted him lightly and laughed. "It's my *hmm, I'm thinking* face."

He laughed. "Ahh, okay. What are you thinking?"

"I just left the auto body shop, and Oliver and Danica are definitely kissing."

His brow wrinkled. "Maybe I missed something. I guess I never heard that Danica and Levi were dating, but I've seen them out by her delivery van being more than friendly. Maybe she flirts with all her customers."

I angled my chin. "Does she with you?"

"Nope. Should I be insulted? I mean, Oliver's a good-looking guy, but Levi? He looks like he should audition for an unkempt pirate. My self-esteem is tanking."

"My attention isn't enough?" I teased.

"Totally enough," he said, brushing a kiss over my lips. "But I'm at least as attractive as Oliver, right?"

I laughed. "More."

Jett pulled a small key from his pocket. "Recognize this?"

"No. Should I?"

"I found it between one of the diner tables and the wall. Where the caulking is? It was in a gap. You should probably have that redone. It's getting old."

"How would you even think to look there? I've never even paid attention to caulking there or anything else."

He winked. "It's my job, baby. And I'm good at it."

The brass key had a thin groove worn along its side, as if it had been used a lot. I turned it in my hand but couldn't place it.

"Do you think it's related to the murder?"

"Not sure. It could have been there for a long time. There's no way to know."

"When did you find it?"

"This morning."

"I didn't know you were at the diner this morning."

"I needed to think, and José's cinnamon rolls were calling to me."

"So you found the key by accident, not skill?"

"Yeah, pretty much."

I pulled out the fake screw and handed it to Jett. "Someone found this in the woods. It's one of Ledford's geocaches. Unscrew the top."

He undid it and pulled out the paper. "A turtle."

"That's a sign from Ledford, I'm almost sure. The turtle at least means it belongs to him, but I think he's sending me a message... or possibly trying to leave a trail for himself. If so, I messed it up."

"And who found this in the woods?"

I exaggerated an eyelash flutter. "Probably José and his friend."

"Ivs..."

"I know. Let's skip the lecture."

He sighed. "I'll send some men out."

"Not Hayes."

"Why?"

"I don't know. He's on my radar. I get checking for someone sneaking around the diner, but why try to open the back door?"

"Hayes is my hardest worker when Ledford isn't around."

"Why don't you go?"

"I'm working on the murder."

"What if it's connected?"

"I haven't seen anything to point to that."

"I point to that." I held up my pointer finger. "And I'm right more than you are."

He frowned. "You're lucky we're on a public street."

I smiled. "Come on. You and me, searching the woods." I ran my hand over his arm.

He kissed me. "I can't. Not today. If things go smoothly, maybe tomorrow."

"But Tania and Ledford could be trapped out there. Tomorrow could be too late."

"I'll send all the workforce I have. Don't worry, alright?"

"Fine. For now."

"Has Tania texted you again?"

"No. I've tried to think of a subtle way to ask if she's in trouble, but I'm coming up blank."

"I haven't heard from Ledford either. I've called every hour. Nothing. And I'm pretty sure Tania already let you know she was in trouble."

"We need to hurry. What if he's hurt? Finding them is more important right now than finding out who killed Elias."

"Unless the killer's still dangerous. I can't leave the town unprotected."

I stared at him, my heart picking up speed. Somewhere out there, Tania and Ledford were waiting—I just hoped they were alive.

Chapter 10

I flopped dramatically onto my bed, hair spilling across my face. I'd spent all day trying—and failing—to figure anything out. Going to bed felt like treason, but passing out from exhaustion wouldn't help anyone.

Creepers climbed onto my stomach and settled in. I was too drained to move him. A sharp bark made me frown—it was way too close not to be inside my place. I lifted my head to find Conan in the doorway.

"What are you doing here?" I asked. He took that as an invitation and bounded over, leaping onto the bed. "Did Boyd forget he dropped you off?"

Conan curled up beside my head. I sighed. "You smell bad."

I turned my head the other way, wondering how I was supposed to sleep with both of them hogging the bed.

It wasn't a worry. I fell asleep almost immediately and didn't move until I heard a pounding on my front door, then Boyd.

"Ivy!" he called. "I lost Conan!"

"He's in here," I croaked. The sun shone through the blinds, but my body didn't want to get up.

Boyd peeked in, and Conan lifted his head.

"There you are. How did you get here?"

"I'm guessing you left him," I said, sitting. Creepers had migrated to my pillow at some point.

"I must be getting old," he muttered. Conan stood and stretched. Boyd picked him up. "Have a good day."

I smiled and shook my head, watching him leave. I got ready quickly and went down to the diner. José and Carrie were already in the kitchen cooking. Carrie looked a little pale.

"Morning," I said. "I'm going to be out most of the day. What do you need me to do?"

"Scrambled eggs," José said. "For two people."

I grabbed a pan, cracked the eggs, and made a few extra for myself. Livy got her order, and I shoveled down mine without caring about the temperature.

"Anything else?" I asked.

"No, I think we're good," José said. "Go ahead."

"You good, Carrie?"

She smiled, but it looked strained. "Yep."

José glanced at Carrie. "Tell her."

Carrie nodded. "I'm pregnant."

I smiled, feeling triumphant for guessing before José. "Congratulations."

"You were right," José said. "We might need to hire someone to help make up the slack when she's sick."

Carrie smiled softly. "José almost freaked out. He's worried people will think he's the grandpa."

"They will," he said, "but I'm still excited. I never thought I would be fifty and a dad."

"You two will be great parents."

"It's going to be an experience."

"Hire anyone you think would work," I told him. "Call me if you need anything."

I went back to the auto body shop, hoping to talk to Levi. Inside, a man with a bushy beard stood behind the counter. I bit back a smile—he did look a bit like a pirate. The skull tattoo on his bicep sealed the deal.

He glared at me. "Oliver said you might show up. I don't know anything."

I offered a smile that felt about as natural as week-old bread. "Did you know Elias well?"

"He worked for me, didn't he?"

That wasn't what I'd asked. "Did he have any enemies that you know of?"

"Nope. I mind my business."

I spotted a roll of twine on the counter. "What's that for?"

His eyes narrowed. "What do you mean? It's twine. We use it to tie up packages."

I thought about the piece we found when Elias was killed. Not that more people couldn't use twine. And it could have been dropped by Elias.

I swallowed, resisting the urge to step back. Definitely not the guy I'd want to run into during a full moon. "Was Elias acting strangely the day he died?"

"Police hire you?"

"No, but it happened in my diner. That makes me nervous."

"Everyone knows about the famous Ivy Clark—always poking her nose into things."

I glared. "And no one cares except people who are guilty."

That wasn't entirely true—the innocent suspects I'd harassed over time probably didn't love it either.

"What would I be guilty of? Killing Elias?" He snorted. "Hardly. I'm not a killer, but if I were, I'd have taken down Oliver a long time ago."

He laughed like it was a joke. I didn't join in.

"If you don't like Oliver, why hire him?"

"Same reason anyone hires anyone around here. They applied. There aren't a lot of choices."

"Did Oliver and Elias get along?"

"Yeah. Now, do you want me to work on your car, or are you going to stay here scaring away the customers?"

I glanced around the empty shop. "I'd hate to do that."

"Great. Leave."

I took a breath and left, almost bumping Danica on the way out. She must help out at the shop a lot. She gave me a curt smile when we moved past each other.

"'Bout time," I heard Levi say. I didn't look back to see if she was giving him the same treatment she gave Oliver. His beard was a little gross, and if she kissed him, it might make me gag.

I went to Jett's next and found Boyd sitting on the lawn playing with Conan. Conan ran over when he saw me, and I scooped him up.

"I'm going into the creepy woods to look for Ledford and Tania."

"Alright," Boyd said, rolling over and struggling to stand. "Put Conan inside and I'll go with you."

I put Conan in the house, and we got in the car.

"I was thinking," Boyd said. "Have you checked all the geocaches in the area where Ledford and Tania went missing?"

"No. Why?"

"I dunno. I just thought they might tell us something."

"Not unless the kidnapper is leaving clues."

"You never know."

"I guess that's true."

"I downloaded the geocaching app to my phone. We can check while we're there."

I pulled onto the main road. "If you want."

"There are several caches in the area. It tells you on the app who made them, and it looks like Ledford made most of them, and he found the others. He's really into this."

When we got to the spot, we went over to the tree where I'd found the first cache.

"You said the geocache here had jewelry?" Boyd asked.

"Yeah."

"And you climbed a tree?"

"Yep."

He looked at his phone. "The clue sounds like it's on the ground, not up the tree."

"No, I didn't climb this tree. That was later, when I was placing a cache." I got down and found the cache. "Here." I opened it and handed it to Boyd.

"Yep, this looks real." He handed it back.

Boyd kicked around the weeds, and I scanned the area. Not that there would be anything new since I'd been here. I placed the box back where it had been.

"Look here," Boyd said, picking up a butter cookie tin. "I bet this is the actual geocache."

He shook it, and something pinged around.

"Why didn't I see that?"

"It was off to the side." He popped off the lid and held it out to me. There were a few little odd things inside, like an eraser, a small toy figure, a jack, and then a paper and pencil.

"So this is the real cache," I muttered, sifting through the things inside. "Then what was that other one?"

"Maybe real jewelry. It was too nice to be costume stuff."

"Who puts jewelry in the woods?"

"Someone who is doing something illegal."

"And Hayes knows something about it. I must have found the one here because it happened to be near a cache. I wonder if Ledford and Tania stumbled onto something they shouldn't have."

"Let's find more of the caches. We might find something else that could help."

I took a deep breath through my nose. I wasn't sure that was our best use of time. It wasn't like whoever hid things out here would hide stuff near all the caches. That would be careless on their part.

"There's one about a quarter of a mile down there," Boyd said, pointing.

I nodded, and we headed that way. I didn't think it would come to anything, but it would get us deeper in the woods. It was a slightly different direction than I'd searched before. After a few minutes, I saw something on the ground.

I squatted down. It looked like an old baseball that had been deflated... but baseballs weren't pumped up. I picked it up and turned it over. It had a small slit on the side. Pulling it open, I found a small piece of paper. My hands trembled as I unfolded it.

"A turtle," I muttered. "It is Ledford. He's leaving clues."

"You might be right."

"He had a bag full of odd things to use as caches. I bet he's dropping them when he can."

We kept going in the direction Boyd's app said since we didn't have any better ideas.

"It should be around here somewhere," Boyd said, gesturing to the surrounding area.

"What's the clue?"

"It's small, don't blink, just stop and think."

"Lovely. Everything here looks the same as everywhere else. That clue stinks."

"It's probably over there by the bushes. At least according to the GPS."

We moved over to the bushes and began moving the branches around. The plant wasn't prickly, but I was still scratching up my arms on the branches.

I saw something and reached as far as I could. I pulled up a cocoa powder container. Geocaching seemed a lot like hiding trash filled with more trash. I took off the yellow lid and looked inside. There was nothing but a ring.

I dumped it out into my hand.

"Mood ring." My heart beat in my ears. "Tania was wearing a mood ring."

"How would she get it in there if she were being watched?"

I rubbed my forehead and tried to think. "Ledford knows where all the geocaches are. Maybe he asked to use the bushes or something and slipped it in."

"I could see that."

I stuck the ring in my pocket.

"The next closest is only about fifty feet," Boyd said. I followed him.

"That rock looks too... something," I said, hurrying past Boyd and picking up a round gray rock. I flipped it over and found a small compartment at the bottom. I opened the fake rock and found another piece of paper with another turtle drawn on it.

"When do we call Jett?" Boyd asked.

"I don't know. Probably ten minutes ago. Let's look for the next cache."

We found it easily, but there was no sign of Ledford or Tania.

"My knee is done," Boyd said. "I need to sit for a while."

"You sit. I'll go find the next one."

Boyd insisted on taking my phone and installing the app so I could see where the caches were hidden, then he settled on a rock and took a drink from his water bottle.

"Call me if anything weird happens," I told him.

"Sure thing."

I followed the directions on my phone, hoping I was going the right way. My heart stopped when I saw movement up ahead. I darted behind a tree, then peeked around.

Hayes. He was about one hundred feet off, looking around. Jett told me he was sending men, so I shouldn't be surprised.

Hayes turned in my direction, and I yanked my head back. It sounded as if someone was running in my direction. What made Hayes zero in on me every time? I turned and ran in the opposite direction. I zigzagged between trees, hoping to lose him. I didn't turn, but I could still hear him.

I swung around a tree—my foot hit loose dirt—and the ground tilted away. My legs shot forward, and I suddenly slid down a slope, branches whipping past. If I died, this was going to sound really stupid in the papers.

Chapter 11

I hit the bottom of the slope hard and sucked in a breath. Pain flared, but nothing felt broken.

"Ivy!" Hayes's voice echoed down after me.

I scrambled to my feet, dirt and twigs clinging to my hair. No time to fix it. No time to think.

"Ivy, come back!"

I bolted into the trees, lungs burning, not daring to look back to see if he was coming after me. It occurred to me that he might only be wondering what I was doing here, but I was too far gone to stop and ask.

I weaved through the trees until I was about to face-plant, then stopped. I bent over, rested my hands on my knees, and breathed deeply. My eyes scanned the area. I reached for my phone, but it was gone.

"Great," I muttered. I had no idea where I was. I wasn't even one hundred percent sure which way I'd come from.

I walked at a fast speed, trying to go the opposite way of Hayes. I couldn't hear him coming. I turned the way I thought the road would be. Boyd better be okay, or I'd never forgive myself. My hand clutched my side, and I slowed down.

Time blurred, and I was almost certain I'd gone the wrong way. Then I spotted it—brown, squat, and hidden in the trees. Not big enough for a house. More like an oversized shed.

I approached quietly and tried to peek in the window. It was too dirty to make anything out, but I could tell a light was on inside. I thought I saw movement, but I wasn't sure if my eyes were playing tricks on me.

I moved slowly to the door and reached out to grab the handle, but I retracted it when I spotted the huge spider. I shook my head. Another of Ledford's geocaches. I would almost bet he and Tania were inside. I tried to turn the handle, but it was locked.

"Tania?" I called.

"Ivy! Is that you?" Tania called back.

"Yes!"

"Hurry! No one's guarding us at the moment."

At least I think that was what she said. Her voice was muffled. I tried slamming into the door with my shoulder, but it was surprisingly solid.

Scanning the ground, I spotted a rock—heavy enough to be useful, light enough to move. I rolled it to the wall beneath the window.

I stepped onto the rock and pushed at the window. It opened with a horrible squeak.

I stuck my head inside. The space was clean but minimal. Several crates sat in one corner. Ledford was tied up in one corner, and Tania in another. I'd never smoothly entered a window, and this drop was a little higher than I was comfortable with. Once I got in, we could use the crates to climb back out.

"Careful," Ledford said. His eye was swollen, and he had a small cut on his cheek.

"We've been here forever!" Tania complained as I pulled myself onto the windowsill. "From what Kaz told me, I thought you would be here the hour we were captured."

Any other time, I would have smiled at Tania calling Ledford Kaz. No one did that.

"At least she's here," Ledford said. "Any backup?"

"Nope. I lost Boyd somewhere. Hayes chased me around for a while. I don't know what side he's on. I have no idea how to get out of the woods because I lost my phone." I put my legs inside and awkwardly jumped to the floor. "Ouch."

I hurried over to Ledford. "You have your phones?"

"No. They took them."

"Why are you going to him first?" Tania whined.

"Because if someone comes in, he'll be more useful." I turned to Ledford. "I'm guessing they took your gun?"

"Yeah."

I moved behind him, stepping over a blue backpack. His hands were tied to a post that went up to the ceiling. I tried to shake the post, but it wouldn't budge.

"Do you have a knife?" Ledford asked.

"In my car."

"How useful."

Tania bristled. "I'm so sick of him, Ivy. All he has is sarcasm and a lot of bad ideas. You have to get me away from him."

I picked at the knot. "Who did this?"

"We don't know," Ledford said, ignoring Tania. "They wore masks and only talked when they had to."

"How many?"

"Two or three. It's hard to tell."

"Kaz let them sneak up on us and get us to move with their guns. We could hear you yelling for us."

"I found the geocaches," I said, making little progress.

"I knew you would," Ledford said. "The men looked in my bag but didn't see anything threatening, so they didn't take anything. I dropped one whenever I could. They walked us all over so they would be sure to have us good and confused."

"I found Tania's ring."

"Oh good," Tania said. "I didn't want to give it to him, but he told me it was necessary. Could you hurry? I'm tired of doing my business in the bushes."

"She never stops complaining," Ledford muttered.

With no warning, the door burst open, and a man in a ski mask pointed a gun at me.

He grumbled something, then a man behind him pushed Boyd in.

"Sit," he said, pointing at an empty post.

I sighed and went over, taking a seat on the wooden floor. The other man put Boyd next to a post and tied him up, then came and did the same to me.

"Why can't you people stay away?" one man said in an obviously disguised voice.

"It figures this is the time you fail," Tania said to me.

"Next time, I'll just leave you."

"Except we're going to die, and there won't be a next time!"

"Any other friends out there?" the taller man asked.

I shook my head. "No."

I studied both of them. I had no clue who they were. One of them was tall and muscular, and possibly Hayes. But why?

"Anyone need a potty break?" the shorter one said.

"I do," Tania said. They cut her ropes, and one grabbed her, pulling her up.

"Remember, run, and we'll shoot your friends."

The shorter one went out with her. I didn't feel confident that Tania would stay for us. She came back, and they took Ledford out. After they pulled out a new rope and tied them back up, they locked the door and left.

"Cozy in here," Boyd said.

Tania glared at him.

Boyd scanned me. "What happened to you? Fight with a dirt monster?"

"More embarrassing. I was running from Hayes, and I fell down a slope. Not gracefully."

"That would explain the nature all over your hair."

I pulled at my ropes.

"It's no use," Ledford said. "Those guys are good at tying knots."

I sighed. I couldn't even move my hands enough to try anything.

"At least we have good company," Boyd offered.

Tania rolled her eyes. "Prison was better than this."

"Any second, I'm going to beg them to throw me in prison to get away from you," Ledford mumbled.

"Prison would suit you."

I glared. "Have you two been fighting all this time?"

Tania tried to toss her hair out of her face. "We take breaks."

"What's in the crates?" I wondered.

"Stolen jewelry and cash," Ledford said. "I've been after these guys for a while. If I'd realized they were camped out here, I wouldn't have chosen this area as part of the geocaching."

"Why did they capture you?"

Tania's gaze flickered to the ground. "I found one of their stashes instead of a geocache."

"What's with the stashes? Why not hide it all here?"

Ledford glanced at me. "My guess? In case someone found this. They didn't want to be left completely empty-handed."

"What are they going to do with us?" Boyd asked. "If they were going to get rid of us, now would be the time."

"My guess? They get all this stuff out and leave us here. They've been taking a little with them every time they come."

"How have you been sleeping tied like this?" I asked.

Tania sniffed. "They tie our hands and feet at night and have us lie on the floor. And they tie our feet to the post so we can't try to help each other escape. Kaz tried to escape last night. That's why he has a black eye."

"Stop calling me Kaz," Ledford muttered.

"Why? It's your name."

"I don't know why I told you."

"It sounds dumb to call people by their last name."

"You can call me Deputy Ledford."

Tania's gaze lingered on him. "What do you have against Kaz?"

"No one calls me Kaz except my immediate family."

"Because you're stuffy?"

"Because it's a stupid name."

"Go by your middle name."

He let out a long sigh. "Not a chance."

"What is it?"

"Why would I tell you? You might start calling me by my whole name."

"I'll guess it."

"Tania," I said. "Knock it off. We need to figure out how to get out of here."

"Seriously," Ledford mumbled. "Be quiet for ten minutes, just for my sanity."

"I will if you tell me your middle name."

He stared at her. "Jedidiah."

"Kaz Jedidiah Ledford?"

"You said you would be quiet."

Tania grinned like she'd just won a battle and leaned against her post.

"I can't believe you two are still sane," I said. "This is so uncomfortable."

"It wasn't so bad before Kaz tried to escape," Tania said. "They tied us tighter after that."

"Your ten minutes aren't up!" Ledford roared.

Tania stared at him with an unrepentant smirk. I couldn't figure her out. Not that it was a new thing. Tania had always been a puzzle.

"We could sing a song," Boyd said. "Help pass the time."

Ledford glared at him.

"Or not."

"There has to be a way out of here," I said, trying not to feel hopeless. "I don't want to miss my wedding because I died here."

"I don't get you and Jett," Tania said, once again proving she couldn't stay quiet. "You two are the weirdest couple."

"They're totally perfect for each other." Ledford scoffed.

Tania raised her brow. "What would you know about it?"

"They have some weird type of storybook love that I never thought actually existed. They love each other, and they sacrifice for each other. It's inspiring in a way."

If my jaw could have hit the floor, it would have. Ledford was actually complimenting me? That might not be the right word, but he was saying things about me, and they were nice.

Tania frowned and blinked a few times. "That kind of love isn't real."

"I didn't think so. Until I saw them. And José and Carrie. I think maybe the problem with the world is that we're all too busy putting ourselves first. If we focus on our wants and needs and ignore other people, we're never happy."

I wasn't sure my mind could comprehend this conversation. I'd never seen this side of Ledford.

Tania looked like someone had just told her dragons exist. "If you always put other people first, you get taken advantage of."

"I'm not saying let people run over you. But maybe we'd be happier if we focused on making someone else happy—" He looked away. "You know what? Let's just drop it."

The room was silent. My eyes scanned it again, and I spotted a scrap of paper near the crates. I stretched my leg out and hooked it closer with my toe. It was part of a torn receipt. I squinted at the signature at the bottom.

"McKay," I read out loud. That could be a first name or a last name... I didn't know.

But it was something.

Chapter 12

"Do you know anyone named McKay?" I whispered to Boyd later that night when we were all trying to sleep.

"Uh... there's a family of McKays down Cherry Blossom Lane."

"How many of them?"

"Parents and two teenage sons. Why?"

I rolled awkwardly, trying to get some of the pressure off my back. "There's a receipt in here. It says McKay. What are they like?"

"The sons are menaces," Ledford butted in. "About eighteen and nineteen."

"Could they be the ones doing this?"

"I suppose. They have similar builds."

A noise at the door made us all go still. Then—*crack!*—the door came off its hinges, splinters flying, and crashed to the floor, missing Boyd by inches.

We all stared at the dark figure in the doorway. No way could we take this guy down, even if we weren't tied up.

The figure's flashlight beam swept over us.

"You all okay?" Jett's voice cut through the shadows as he rushed in.

"There's a light by the door," I told him, my heart trying to calm down.

He flipped it on and went straight to Ledford, pulling a knife and slicing through the ropes. Ledford sat up, rubbing his wrists.

Jett handed him a gun. "Keep that on the door."

Ledford turned toward the empty doorway while Jett cut his feet loose.

When Jett came toward me, I jerked my head toward Tania. "Get her first. She's been tied up the longest. Then Boyd."

Jett freed Tania, then Boyd, before finally coming back to me.

I smiled. "Told you they were here."

"Yeah, Miss Smartypants. You were right."

"How did you find us?"

"I figured you were out here, so I called in police from another city. They're all over the woods looking for you guys and the baddies."

Tania glared. "When we go missing, Ivy and Boyd come. But when Ivy goes missing, she gets the royal treatment?"

"I didn't think you two were out here. Since Ledford's car turned up in town, I figured you were somewhere else."

Ledford nodded. "One of the men took the car. He said if people saw it around town, people would think we were just avoiding people, not missing."

Boyd snorted. "Half the town thinks the two of you ran off together."

Ledford shuddered.

Tania wrinkled her nose. "Eww."

Jett pulled me to my feet, and I tipped against him. He put his arm around me. "Let's get out of here."

"How did you know we were here?" Boyd asked.

"And," Tania added, "if you thought we were here, why did you kick the door down so hard?"

"I figured you were here when I saw it. I don't know when the captors would come back, so I was trying to be fast."

"You could have killed us with the door."

"But I didn't. I didn't need the flashlight to know you were here. I smelled you all before I saw you."

I poked him in the ribs. "Punk. Let's hurry."

We stepped into the dark woods, and the air felt heavier, thicker, like it was holding its breath. Shadows twisted between the trees, and every rustle made me wonder if we were being followed. An owl in the trees almost made me scream.

Jett called to let the other officers know he'd found us and to keep searching for the men.

"Let's go quickly and quietly," Jett said.

I took his hand, and we speed-walked through the trees. My eyes kept darting to the black gaps between trunks, and I tried—really tried—not to listen to the low crack of branches somewhere off to our left.

A deafening boom split the night, the ground trembling beneath us. We all spun toward the sound.

Flames licked up into the darkness, casting the trees in a flickering orange glow.

"What was that?" Tania gasped.

"The shed," Jett said grimly. "They blew it up—along with all the evidence. Dang it."

"Should I go back?" Ledford asked.

"No. We get everyone safe first," Jett said, already steering us away from the blaze. He made a few calls while we moved, but I wasn't listening.

A bullet sliced through the trees, and we all dropped. Jett and Ledford rolled onto their stomachs, guns aimed into the darkness.

"Get them out," Jett ordered.

Ledford nodded, getting to his feet. "Come on, hurry."

"I'm not leaving you here," I said.

"Go, Ivs. I need to concentrate."

I swallowed my protest and followed Ledford with Tania and Boyd. I wasn't okay with it, but I didn't want to be the reason Jett got distracted.

The woods rustled—too close. A dark figure burst from the shadows, tackling Ledford.

Before I could react, Tania darted forward, snatched his fallen gun, and swung it like a baseball bat. The crack of metal against skull was so loud it made my teeth ache.

The man crumpled to the ground.

I froze. "Tania...?"

She didn't answer, just shoved the gun back into Ledford's hands.

Jett was suddenly there, hauling the man upright and cuffing him.

Ledford stared at Tania as if she'd grown an extra head.

Boyd let out a low whistle. "Nice hit."

Tania grinned, breathless. "I've never done anything like that before."

Ledford gave a half-smile. "I'm glad you did. Thanks."

Tania didn't bother with a simple "you're welcome." She flung herself at him and kissed him—full Tania-style. Tania never did anything halfway, and this kiss looked like it might give Ledford a heart attack.

Even the attacker stopped to stare—although he might have just been dazed from the blow to the head.

Jett shook his head, then led the man forward.

Tania pulled back. Ledford's eyes were huge.

"We never talk about this again," she said.

"Never," he said quickly.

Thankfully, Jett knew where we were, so he led us out to where several cop cars were parked right by my car.

He yanked the man's mask off to reveal… someone I'd never seen before. The man scowled, and Ledford handed him a towel from his car. He pressed it to his bleeding head without a word.

"Drive Boyd and Tania straight to town," Jett told me. "I need to talk to everyone, but it might take a while to get around to it."

I nodded but didn't start the car until Jett had the man locked in the back of his truck.

We drove for two minutes in silence before Boyd coughed in the back seat. "So… Tania and Ledford?"

"No!" Tania snapped. "That was an adrenaline kiss. Those don't count."

Boyd chuckled. "Whatever you say."

Tania turned to the window, crossing her arms. "Still… you should feel the muscles in that guy's back. If he shaved and grew a few inches, there might be something there."

I rolled my eyes. Tania would always be Tania.

"Did you recognize the man?" I asked.

"Nope," Boyd said.

"Me neither," Tania replied.

I chewed my lip. I needed to get home to Creepers. He probably hadn't missed me, but Conan would have missed

Boyd by now... although Jett probably fed him. I dropped Boyd off, then drove quietly home.

Tania and I went up the back steps and inside. Creepers sat by the door, tail twitching, and gave me an annoyed meow. I hurried to the kitchen and filled his bowl. He glared at me before eating.

"You're fine. Missing dinner by a few hours never hurt anyone."

"He looks like he could miss a meal and be fine," Tania said. "He's kinda fat. You shouldn't overfeed animals."

"I only give him what's recommended. He's not over-weight."

Tania flopped into a chair and sighed. "I need a cookie."

"The jar's right there." I pointed at it.

Tania gave me a flat stare that clearly meant she wanted me to bring it to her. I got a glass of water instead. I wasn't letting Tania intimidate me—that was me in a different life.

Tania sighed, got a drink, grabbed a cookie, and sat back down.

The clock said it was 1:00 a.m., but Tania didn't look like she was going to bed. I sat across from her and ignored the throbbing in my wrists. Tania's had to feel a lot worse.

"I can't believe I kissed Kaz," Tania said between bites. "That was totally out of character for me."

Not true, but it wasn't the time for an argument. "I still find it weird you call him Kaz."

"I like it. It's fun."

"If you say so. And I think you almost put him into shock when you kissed him."

She laughed. "Everyone needs a little shock in their lives. And the weird thing is, my heart actually sped up. Don't ever tell him that. He was barely even kissing me back, and I still enjoyed it. It would have been better if he hadn't had a mustache."

"I can't comprehend this. I'm going to bed."

She shoved the rest of the cookie in her mouth and stood. "Me too. And tomorrow, I'm gonna ask Kaz to shave."

I shook my head. "Don't."

Chapter 13

It might not be usual, but Jett and Ledford sat in my living room while Jett prepared to question Tania and me. I was usually interviewed in the sheriff's office. The two of us sat on the couch, and they sat on kitchen chairs facing us.

"Who was the guy?" I asked Jett.

"He won't say. He claims he wasn't in on the kidnapping. Said he's just a delivery guy."

"Do you believe him?"

"I don't know yet. He's not giving me much to go on. He did shoot at us, so he's not going free."

Ledford was avoiding eye contact with everyone.

"Kaz, have you ever thought about shaving?" Tania blurted out, like it was a normal conversation.

Ledford blinked. "No."

"What's with the mustache? Too lazy to shave? You don't like it, do you?"

He touched his mustache and glared.

Tania leaned forward. "The only person who can pull off a mustache is Tom Selleck."

Ledford crossed his arms and didn't say anything.

"Let's get back on topic," Jett said.

Tania rolled her eyes. "Why do we even have to do this? Kaz was with me the entire time. I'm sure he told you everything he knows."

I looked at Ledford. "Did you tell Jett about the receipt?"

"No. I'm so tired, I haven't been thinking straight."

"What receipt?" Jett asked.

"I saw one in the shed. It said McKay."

"My bet is it's those two McKay boys," Ledford told Jett. "They've been in enough trouble to make it believable."

"They sure have."

"You want me to talk to them?"

"Not alone. And you should probably rest today. You've been through a lot."

"I'm fine. I'll go grab one of the others and take them with me."

"Sounds good."

Ledford left, and Tania's eyes followed him. "He's confident."

"I can't believe you insulted his mustache," I said. "Who does that? He should be allowed to have whatever facial hair he wants."

Jett grinned and ran a hand over his stubble. "Should he now?"

I glared at him, but my mouth twitched. "I never told you how to wear your facial hair."

"But I still got the message."

"Through Boyd."

Tania's brows came together. "You told Boyd your preference in facial hair? And you think I'm odd?"

"I didn't... It just slipped out, okay?"

"And you like that?" she asked, pointing at Jett. He just grinned. "I mean, it's like what a guy does when he's lazy. Shave every few days. I hope he shaves for your wedding."

"I'll shave tonight," he said. "Then I'll be ready."

Tania rolled her eyes. "Then you'll look just like you do now by the wedding."

I smiled. "And that's how I like it."

Tania shook her head as if she felt sorry for me. "To each their own. I'm still tired. Can't we do this later?"

"I guess," Jett said. "Come by the station after your morning nap."

Tania stood and went to the guest room.

"You ready?" Jett asked.

"For what?"

His eyes sparkled. "Being interrogated."

I raised my brows. "Interrogated? Am I a suspect? I'm pretty sure I couldn't have tied myself up like that."

He laughed. "Okay, questioned."

"Not really what I want to do. I don't have anything helpful to add. I didn't see anyone's face. I failed yesterday. I couldn't even save us. Tania was more helpful than I was."

Jett moved over to the couch. "You can't be the hero every time."

"Yeah, well, I don't like to be the one getting rescued."

"I need to rescue you occasionally. I'm the sheriff, and you've rescued me more than I have you. It's bad for my self-esteem when it happens too much." He pulled me over and kissed my cheek.

"I thought you were questioning me?" I said, wrapping my arms around him.

"I am." He kissed me lightly. "First question, why did you go out there when I told you not to? You could have gotten killed." He kissed me again.

"Do you really want my answer? It's not like you don't know."

"That you can't control yourself when anything illegal happens?" Another kiss.

"I am not being questioned like this," I said as he kissed the corner of my mouth.

"It's way more fun."

I rubbed my hands over his prickly face. "I don't like to multitask." I pulled his face closer and kissed him firmly, not wanting to mess around with his teasing.

"I'm still in the apartment," Tania said, peeking in.

"Kind of unfortunate," Jett said, not releasing me. His lips were right back on mine, and I heard Tania huff and walk away.

Tania didn't have room to talk. She'd kissed Ledford in front of all of us. This was my place, and she was supposedly taking a nap.

I pulled away and settled my head against his chest. "Don't you have work to do?"

"Yeah, but you aren't letting me do it."

"I love you."

He rubbed his hand over my back. "I love you. I really should go get something done. You go rest."

"I need to go help in the diner."

"I'm surprised you haven't been chasing the murderer harder. Not that I'm complaining."

"I know. I want to, but I'm not motivated. I was determined to find Ledford and Tania, but now... I just want to get married and not worry about things like Elias Prescott."

"Good. You focus on the wedding, and I'll focus on Elias."

As I stood so he could go, he smirked. "Besides, I'm still perfecting the art of questioning you with kisses. Can't let that skill go to waste."

"Is it a skill, though?" I teased.

"I think so."

We might have kissed for another five minutes before I finally made my way down to the diner. I felt a twinge of guilt. Jett was right. I wasn't giving poor Elias the attention I usually would. Someone needed to figure out what had happened to him.

I walked into the kitchen to find all my cooks scurrying around.

"Sorry," I said. "I am completely unmotivated. What do you need?"

"Jett told us what happened," José said. "You should be resting."

"I'm fine."

"We need a pan of something for Barbra's book club tonight," Carrie said.

"Right. I lost track of the days. I'll make something."

I pulled out the mixer and tried to remember what I'd made last time. Probably cookies. So brownies it was. I reached for the sugar canister and frowned—someone had scribbled a phone number in pencil on the lid. It was partially erased, but the first three digits were from out of state. I didn't recognize the number, but for some reason it made me think of that torn "McKay" receipt. Another thing to add to my mental list for Jett.

I wrote down the number, squinting hard to see the part that was rubbed.

I went back to measuring flour, my mind wandering—last night, Elias, and Jett's lips. The last one made me smile. The middle one made me frown.

I put the brownies in the oven and reached for my phone to set a timer. Right—I'd lost it. Probably when I fell down that slope. The chances of my finding that exact spot were slim.

The back door opened a crack, and Ledford's voice came through. "Ivy? Can you come out here?"

"Sure." I brushed off my apron and stepped outside. Ledford stood there. No mustache.

"Really? You gave in to Tania?"

"I know, I know. But what if she was right? What do you think?"

I smiled, not used to Ledford looking uncertain—especially when talking to me. "It looks good."

"Better?"

"Yes, but if you like it, grow it back."

"I don't really care much about my appearance."

"You don't want to impress Tania, do you?"

He rubbed his head. "I don't know. I'm not the kind of guy girls like her pursue. Or... any girls, really."

I hesitated. Ledford wasn't bad-looking, but his personality was prickly. "Tania isn't exactly the safest dating option. You might want to be careful."

"All we did was fight until you found us—but it was almost... fun. Then she kissed me? Wow. But I know I'm not her type. I don't know what to do."

"Are you coming to me for relationship advice? Because if you are, that's really weird."

"I know. But I don't have any friends. Who else should I talk to?"

I nodded. "We've been through a lot. I think we count as friends by now."

He smiled slightly.

The door to my apartment opened, and Tania came out—short skirt, button-up shirt, and as much makeup as I wear in a month. She bounced down the stairs humming... until she saw us.

She froze. Her eyes went wide at Ledford. A hand flew to her neck. "You shaved."

Ledford shifted. Shrugged.

"Because I told you to?"

"It was probably time," he mumbled.

"Wow. It looks... wow."

Ledford didn't seem to know which leg to stand on. The silence stretched, and I didn't know if etiquette required me to stay for whatever this was.

Tania combed her fingers through her hair. Ledford cleared his throat.

"I don't do awkward," Tania announced.

"What?" Ledford asked.

She stepped forward—and this time, Ledford was ready. He wrapped her in his arms, and the kiss that followed was something I sincerely hoped I could erase from my memory. I was pretty sure I'd just been dismissed.

I went back into the diner and checked my timer. The smell of brownies was taking over the kitchen—not a bad thing.

"What's that look for?" Carrie asked.

"What look?" I shook my head, trying to come back to the present.

"You look amused and disgusted at the same time."

I laughed. "I am. Ledford and Tania are out back, ugly kissing."

"Seriously?" Anton dropped his spoon onto the spoon rest. "Alright, folks, we're going live." He slid to the curtain and pulled it back just enough to peek. "And we have... ooh gross. Really gross."

José joined him. "Oof. That's a lot of teeth."

"They'd make a terrible couple," Anton said, still watching. "Are they done? Oh, she's going in for a second round."

"Leave them alone," Carrie scolded. "You want people spying on you when you're doing that?"

José grinned. "I wouldn't mind. We have mad kissing skills. Those two? They look like they're just learning where their lips are."

Carrie tossed a rag at him, but José ducked. "Okay, okay—hold up. She just tilted her head. He's adjusting. This could be the turning point, folks."

Anton chuckled. "Oh no. False alarm. They just bonked noses."

José winced. "Penalty."

I held in a giggle. They didn't need any encouragement.

"Wait, wait, there we go," Anton said. "They slowed down. They're figuring out their game."

"Alright, enough," Carrie said, yanking the curtain shut.

Anton sighed. "Shame. I think they might get it right."

"You two are ridiculous," Carrie said, stirring something in a pot.

Livy came in and clipped an order on the bulletin board.

"Hey, Liv," Anton said. "Peek out that window."

"Don't do it," Carrie said.

Livy smiled slightly. "What's going on?"

"Just look. It's hilarious."

Livy moved over to the window and peeked out. "Oh my. Is that... oh my." She dropped the curtain. "Please tell me I've never looked like that."

Anton grinned. "I can't say. I've never seen you kiss anyone from a distance."

"And you never will."

He winked at her. "Good."

I smiled. Inside, Anton and Livy were young, in love, and adorable. Outside, Ledford and Tania... well, they were something.

Chapter 14

I stood in front of the auto body shop and peered through the glass door. Levi leaned against the counter inside, and I wasn't thrilled about going in again. After talking to half the town and getting nothing but 'Elias kept to himself,' I figured this place was still my best option.

I stepped inside. Levi glanced up, his lip swollen and one eye a little puffy.

"What now?" he grumbled.

My eyes narrowed. "Did Elias have a girlfriend?" It was something I hadn't thought to ask until now—and I really wished Oliver were here to do the answering. He was easier to talk to.

"Not really," Levi said.

"What does that mean?"

"It means he hung out with Danica when she came around, but they weren't dating."

My opinion of Danica slid down another notch. She just stopped by the shop to make out with whoever wasn't busy? I'd heard weirder... but not much.

"And that didn't bother you?"

"What?"

"That he and Danica—"

He laughed. "Danica doesn't know what she wants. Figuring her out is impossible."

"But I thought you and Danica—"

"What?" He cut me off again. "Thought we were together? Nah. Danica ain't picky. She'll spend a few playful minutes with anyone."

"And you're all cool with that?"

"Why not? It's boring around here. Course, Elias was gone on Danica more than the rest of us. It irritated him that he wasn't the only one she was hanging around."

My interest piqued. "Oh?"

"He started buggin' her, trying to get her to date him, but she wasn't having any of it. They had a big fight last week. She feels awful about it now."

Awful didn't equal innocent.

"And she doesn't like any of you more than the others? Isn't that weird to you?"

"Nah. You can follow her on her deliveries. That woman has problems. Bet she treats most of the men on her routes the same way she does here. She'd probably calm down if that lawman would pay her some attention. She sure lights up when he's around."

My stomach dropped like a stone. Heat prickled up my neck, a mix of suspicion and something I refused to call jealousy. "Which lawman?"

"Don't care to know their names. Tall, curly-haired pretty boy."

"Hayes?" It had to be Hayes. He was the only one with curly hair.

"That's it."

"Look what I found!" a man called, coming in the back way. He spotted me, froze, and immediately shoved whatever he'd been about to show behind his back. I didn't recognize him.

Levi's glare could have peeled paint.

"You work here?" I asked.

The man glanced at Levi like he needed permission to answer.

"He doesn't work here," Levi muttered. "He's my brother."

I blinked. The brother was... different. Clean clothes, tidy hair, no fuzzy beard. He looked like he actually owned a comb.

Without another word, he walked behind the counter and dropped whatever he'd been holding into something that clanged like a metal bin.

Oliver came in the front and smiled. "Hey, Miss Clark."

I smiled back. "Hi, Oliver."

"Miss Clark seems to be awfully interested in Danica and her relation to this shop," Levi said.

Oliver laughed. "Who wouldn't be? I keep saying we should ban her. It might be the only way we'd ever get any work done."

I made a mental note to never bring my car here.

"I'm out of here," Levi said, handing a key ring to Oliver. Levi and his brother left.

"Working for Levi must be great fun," I said, my voice thick with sarcasm.

"Man, no. Levi's a jerk, but I need a job, and I'm good at this. I'm just happy we don't have to work together too often."

"What happened to his face?"

"I didn't notice anything, but I don't make it a point of staring at him."

"I'm still stuck on the Danica thing."

He sighed. "It's a problem. I feel bad for her. She must be lonely."

"You almost seem like a decent guy, and then miss it completely when it comes to her."

He scratched his head. "Yeah, I know. I work here, then do side jobs from home. No time for a life. So when she comes in... I don't know. I know it's messed up. All of it."

Oliver looked down and picked something up. "Someone threw a phone in the garbage."

I squinted at it. "That's mine."

He handed it to me. "Did you hear about whatever happened in the woods last night?" he asked. "Crazy."

"Yeah, it really was."

"Right. You would know. You and the sheriff and all."

"I was there."

"Ooh. Glad you didn't get hurt."

"Thanks."

"I heard they arrested five people."

"Five? I only heard one."

"You're probably right. Rumors run fast. Some kind of jewelry smuggling, I hear? That's an odd thing to smuggle."

"Yeah. I need to go. Thanks for talking to me."

I walked out, clutching the phone. It still had mud along the edges, and the battery was nearly dead. If Levi's brother found it, that meant he'd been in the woods—exactly where I'd dropped it when I fell down the slope. And if he'd been there, what else had he seen? Or done?

Danica could wait. I needed to find Jett.

I went right across to the station, hoping he was there. He was, and so was Ledford.

"Anything on the McKays?" I asked.

"The parents said they weren't home," Ledford said. "I'm pretty sure they were lying."

I glanced at Hayes, who was sitting at a computer. "Can we go to your office?"

"Sure." Jett led me, and Ledford followed. I shut the door and turned to Ledford. "When you were in that fight the other night, did you punch the guy in the mouth?"

He grinned. "Sure did. If there weren't two of them, I would have won."

"Levi Calloway has a fat lip. And his brother came into the shop and tossed my phone in the trash. It got lost in the woods last night. They're part of it."

Jett nodded. "I'll go to the shop."

"He isn't there. He left about ten minutes ago."

"Anything else?"

"Danica is a... floozy."

Ledford snorted, and Jett smiled.

"A what now?" Jett asked.

I punched him on the arm. "Don't make fun of me. She goes to the auto shop and makes out with whoever's working."

"Along with half the town," Ledford said. "It's common knowledge."

"I didn't know. Also, she lied to me. She said she saw Ledford and Tania leave the diner when they were tied up in the woods. Ledford's car being gone just proves it wasn't them — someone else moved it to make her story look real. I think Levi is the man behind the smuggling, and he got

Danica to lie for him, to throw us off. And his brother probably works for him."

Jett nodded. "That sounds pretty solid. What do you think?"

Ledford rubbed his chin. "Very likely. But what about the McKays?"

"The McKays are always up to something. Probably something else this time. Or maybe they help make deliveries?"

"So what do we do?" I asked.

Jett turned to me. "You take your cute little self to the diner, and Ledford and I will deal with this."

I couldn't think of a single reason I shouldn't do that, so I walked back to the diner.

I was pretty much useless at the diner. I whisked something José handed me and paced. I told José, Carrie, and Anton about my suspicions, and they all thought it was probably right.

I went to the event room and sat in the back, watching Barbra conduct her book club.

"Boyd, if you can't say anything nice, I'm putting you on a ten-minute time-out," she was saying.

Boyd sat back in his chair. "I'm not allowed to have an opinion?"

Barbra glared at him. "You can have an opinion, but you can't tell other people that theirs is stupid."

"Anyone who thinks that book qualifies as good literature is crazy."

"That's it. No talking from you for ten minutes."

He sighed, and Opal clapped.

"It's about time," she said. "I think we should let Boyd choose the next book, then criticize his choice."

"Please, let me choose," Boyd said.

Barbra glared at him, and he closed his mouth.

Book club didn't have the vibe I wanted tonight. I hadn't seen Tania in a while, so I went upstairs to check on her. When I opened the door, I saw her quickly move Creepers from her lap. I hid a smile. He was growing on her.

"How's it going?" I asked.

"Fine."

"You think it might be good to go look for a job or something?"

"Nope. I mean, I do have to get a job soon, but with the money from my mom's house, I should be set for a while."

"Are you staying around here?"

"I don't know. I might want to start over somewhere new. Where people don't know my past."

"That might be good."

"The only thing is... I don't even know how to comprehend this. Kaz is getting under my skin. Being the same height actually makes kissing convenient. He's a really good kisser."

I smiled, remembering Anton's and José's commentary. "You don't get along."

"We probably could. I've never dated a guy who was… What's the word? Normal?"

I laughed. "Ledford is not normal."

"I mean, he's not a creep or a thief or anything."

"You have had some sad relationships."

"After we finished kissing, we kind of awkwardly went our own ways. I wanted to say something, but I couldn't think of anything. That's not like me. I think this could be the real thing."

"Slow down," I cautioned. "You hated him yesterday."

"So? You know I'm impulsive. He shaved his freaking mustache for me. That says something."

Chapter 15

I opened the front door of Jett's house. Boyd had texted to ask for help with something. As soon as I came in, Conan ran up to me barking and jumping.

"Hey, pal. Where's Boyd?"

"In here!" Boyd called.

I followed his voice upstairs and stopped in the doorway. Boyd isn't thin, but he looked much bigger than usual, and he could barely put his arms down.

"What's going on?"

"I was trying to set a record for the most shirts a man over seventy could put on at once. I couldn't get any more on, and now I can't get them off. I made my back sore."

"Boyd, only you would do something like this. Why?"

"I know. I'm too old. Got it, but I can't live my life in a boring way."

I tugged on the top shirt, but it kept rolling. "How many do you have on?"

"Don't know. Lost track. At least fifty."

"Boyd, you don't even own fifty shirts."

He lifted his arms straight out. "Can't get them higher."

"This is absurd."

"Hello?" José called from downstairs.

"Up here!" I yelled.

José came over and shook his head. "Bad move, Boyd."

"I know that now."

José pulled out his phone and snapped a picture.

"Hey!" Boyd cried. "You didn't let me smile." He smiled, and José took another picture.

"As the mayor of Muddy Creek, this is good blackmail," José said.

"I don't care about stuff like that. The mayor stuff is such a joke. I thought I'd actually be busy, but nope. Four hours a week."

"If that's as high as you can get it, we're going to have to cut some of them off," I said, going to the kitchen and grabbing Jett's scissors.

"No cutting any of the Hawaiian shirts," Boyd instructed.

"I'll try, but the top layers have to go."

"The Hawaiian shirts are button-up, so they should come off easier."

I began cutting. After the first ten, there was a button-up, so José undid that one and took it off.

"What in the world are you guys doing?" Jett asked, entering with Conan barking at his heels.

"Boyd put on fifty shirts and had to call for help," José said.

Jett chuckled. "Typical day in the life of Boyd Webster."

"Someone should tell this story at my funeral. I want people laughing, not crying. My life is full of annoying yet hilarious stories."

"That's for sure," I said. "Can you raise your arms more?"

"Nope. Not with my back. I might not be able to raise them at all."

I looked at Jett. "Your scissors are awful."

He held out his hand. "I'll do some."

I handed him the scissors, and he started cutting. "Want to hear the news?"

"You know I do."

"We arrested Levi and his brother. That little key in the diner? It fit in a lockbox at Levi's house, full of jewelry. This might be one of the biggest jewelry rings Kansas has ever seen. And not only that, Levi sent a text telling Elias to sneak into the diner to look for the key."

"So that's why Elias was in there. And Levi knew he was in there."

"Yep. Elias was working with Levi. We found bank records proving he was paying Elias more than just his salary. Several other people were involved, but not from Muddy Creek."

"What about Oliver?"

"He wasn't on the records, aside from his normal paycheck."

"I wish I had figured out the key," I said, accidentally out loud.

"Hey," Jett said. "Don't you want me to do my job? You can't solve everything. Don't steal my thunder, woman."

I smiled slightly. "But I haven't figured anything out this time."

"That's not true. You figured out Levi and his brother were behind it."

"Not with real evidence. Only guesses."

"Good ones."

"And you found Ledford and Tania and where things were being stored."

"But it got blown up."

"There were remnants left."

"Do you think Levi killed Elias?"

"There's no proof, but my guess is he did. When we talked to the brother, he said Levi was irritated that Danica was spending more time with Elias."

"Great," I said, sitting on the couch. "That means we can get married with nothing in the way."

"Yep. That's what it looks like."

"That's good," Boyd said. "I'm getting tired. We can get the rest off tomorrow."

"You're going to sleep in all those shirts?" Jett asked. "You'll overheat. Just hang on and I'll go faster."

"I'm going to take off if you don't need me," José said. "I got my picture."

"That's fine," Jett said.

"I'm going as well. I don't want an angry cat again tonight." I went out and climbed into my car. I drove around the corner and saw a van with "Danica's Delivery" on the side.

Going home was probably smart, but I followed at a distance.

She made a few fast deliveries, then drove to a house. I didn't know who lived there, but she got out, straightened her skirt, and ran her fingers through her hair. I parked a few houses down. She went around the house, so it must be a basement apartment. Those were common in Muddy Creek.

I got out of my car and went around the other side of the house so I wouldn't run into her. I poked my head around the back and watched her go down a few stairs and knock.

The door opened, and Hayes came out, shutting the door behind him.

"Hey, Danica," he said. He crossed his arms. "I didn't need any deliveries."

"I just wondered if you weren't happy with my deliveries? You used to have me get your groceries every week."

Hayes shrugged. "I decided to stop being lazy and get my own stuff."

"Ahh." She smiled. "I miss talking to you."

He pursed his lips. "It was nice to see you. I'll talk to you later."

"Wait!" She grabbed his arm. "You don't have to go in."

He yanked his arm away. "I do. Please leave."

Her lips went out in a pout. "What is it you don't like about me?"

"I've made it clear several times that I'm not interested in being one of your 'stops.' You make me uncomfortable."

She looked angry, then smiled. "But I know what you did. Do you want that getting out?"

He went stiff. "Goodbye, Danica." He went in and shut the door.

Great. Now I would have to wonder what Hayes did. I ran around the house so I would meet Danica in the front. She came around and stopped when she spotted me.

"You keep popping up everywhere," she said.

I gave a tight smile. "I was thinking the same about you."

"Yeah, I get around."

"Did you hear about Levi?"

She frowned. "Yeah. That's going to hurt me. I make a lot of money from the guys at the auto body shop by buying their groceries and moving their auto parts. I hope Oliver can keep the shop running."

"Can I ask you a question?"

"Sure."

"You told me you saw Tania and Ledford leave the diner. That was impossible because they were tied up in the woods. Why did you lie?"

She twitched, then her expression went neutral. "I thought I saw them. Must have been someone who looked similar."

"You grew up in Muddy Creek, and you're close to Tania's age. I doubt you mistook someone for her."

She scowled. "I don't have to explain anything to you." She moved past me and went to her car.

"The police will eventually want to know," I said to her back. "It's going to look like you were trying to cover something."

She spun around. "It was an honest mistake, okay? I've been having a bad week. First, Elias dies, then Levi and Gabe get arrested. I was friends with all of them. And now you're accusing me of things?"

"Is Gabe Levi's brother?"

"Yeah."

"You lied. I might be accusing you, but you did."

"Look, I don't know anything, okay? Levi paid me to tell you I saw them. I didn't know why, and I didn't ask."

"Dangerous way to live your life."

"Tell me about it. Now, are we done?"

"Did Levi kill Elias?"

She laughed angrily. "Why would I know that?"

"You seem close to everyone in the shop."

"And you think they're going to tell me if they decide to kill each other? Would I be shocked if Levi killed Elias? Not if he'd done it the day before he died."

I wrinkled my forehead. "What?"

"I had a special relationship with all the men there. The day before he died, Elias told me he was done with me." Her eyes narrowed as she remembered. "I think it's because they were starting to have issues at the shop. Fighting. Jealousy. Levi is the most attached to me, and he threatened to fire the others if they didn't break things off with me. Elias did. Oliver wouldn't."

"But he didn't get fired?"

"Levi knows he needs workers, and it's hard to find people to work there. Levi and Oliver had a huge fight. If Levi was going to kill anyone, it would have been Oliver. I was mad at everyone. I didn't stick around to see what happened," Danica said, arms crossed. "But the next day, they all acted normal. Then Elias turned up dead."

I had no proof, but it only made me more sure that Levi killed him. If they were already fighting, and Levi sent Elias to the diner, he could've followed him. But why kill him before he found the key?

"I heard you were the one who broke things off with Elias."

"That's a lie. I liked Elias better than a lot of guys. I have an order, and Levi was at the bottom. Especially of the guys in the shop. Now, will you excuse me?"

"Thanks for talking," I said, though she'd given me more questions than answers.

She slid into her car without looking back.

I drove home, head buzzing. Creepers greeted me at the door, and I curled onto the couch with him. Tania must already be in bed.

It had to be Levi—the smuggling, the murder. But then again... Danica had admitted she was furious when Elias broke things off. I needed to keep better notes. I was forgetting who said what, and what I was thinking. It must be the wedding. I couldn't concentrate on anything fully, so my mind was messy.

I stroked Creepers's head. "Ready for bed?"

He meowed.

"Me too."

Chapter 16

"Sleeping in? The day before your wedding?"

I sat up and turned to see my mom and dad standing in my doorway. I rubbed my eyes, and Creepers ran out the door.

I yawned. "I didn't expect you this early. How did you get in?"

"The door wasn't locked. Sorry we couldn't come earlier," Mom said. "I bet you have a lot to get done. What do you need us to do?"

"Not a lot. I bought everything a while back, and José's going to make the cake today. All we need to do is decorate the church."

"Great. I've been waiting your whole life for this!"

Dad laughed. "You'd better give your mom something to do."

"Can I shower first?"

"I suppose," Mom said. "We'll go downstairs and have breakfast."

"How was your flight?"

"Too early, but fine. We'll see you when you come down."

I got ready for the day, then met them. Mom wanted to decorate the church, so we took all the decorations over, and she started with Carol and a few of their friends. My mom grew up here, so she knows most of the town. They kicked me out, telling me they wanted to surprise me.

I ended up standing in the middle of town, wondering why sidewalks lately made me feel helpless.

"Ivs!" Jett called, jogging over to me. "I've been looking all over for you, and you didn't answer your phone."

"I left it at home."

"What do we need to do?"

I shrugged. "Our moms took over decorating, and the cake is in progress. Did you pick up your tux?"

"Yes, last night. I'm never using that shop again. I don't know what makes that little clerk think he's so high and mighty. I've got nothing to do, so boss me."

"I feel like we should be really busy, but it's all taken care of."

"You mean I took an extra day off so we could do nothing?"

"Maybe."

"Great. I could use a boring day."

"Want me to tell you what Danica told me yesterday first?"

He let out a breath. "Not really, but you probably should."

"What if we go to the B&B and soak in the hot tub while I tell you?" I'm not a big hot tub person, but Jett loves to soak while he's thinking.

His grin spread wide. "That I can get behind."

Fifteen minutes later, we were in the hot tub, and Jett already looked relaxed enough to sleep. His head rested against the concrete ledge, eyes closed.

"Alright, tell me about Danica."

I told him everything, from her scene with Hayes to the fights at the auto shop.

"What do you think?" I asked.

"I still think Levi killed Elias, but I should talk to Danica. If she were mad enough, it could've been her. And I don't love how she's running her 'business.' Makes the town look bad."

"I can't believe she's never tried anything with you. I was embarrassed for her with Hayes. And she's obviously not picky if she hangs out with Levi."

He cracked an eye and grinned. "So you're saying she should hit on me because she's not picky?"

I splashed water at him. "You know that's not what I mean. You're way hotter than any guy she hangs out with."

"Perhaps she has some standards—if not many. She knows we're engaged."

"Maybe. Hayes definitely shut her down."

"I'm glad. I don't want my officers tangled up in things like that."

"What about her comment that she knew something about Hayes?"

"Could be anything. I'm ready to turn it all over to Ledford for the next two weeks."

"I heard you two were here," Boyd said, strolling in wearing blue-and-white flower swim trunks. He puffed out his chest like he was about to enter a swimsuit competition.

Jett tilted his head. "Perfect timing, Boyd. I was just thinking, 'You know what this pre-wedding soak with my fiancée needs? Boyd in floral swim trunks.'"

"Well, someone had to make it memorable," he said, easing into the hot tub.

I smiled, and Jett shook his head.

"I want your key, Boyd," Jett said.

Boyd blinked. "To your house?"

"No. The one to Ivy's apartment. No more surprise visits."

"He plays with Creepers," I cut in. "Creepers loves him."

Jett pinched the bridge of his nose. "Fine. But I'm getting a chain lock."

Boyd grinned. "As long as I still get visitation rights, I'll allow it."

"What if we set hours?" Jett suggested. "You're only allowed between 10 a.m. and 2 p.m."

"That's when I usually go anyway. Just a warning, Ivy—this guy doesn't know how to clean a bathroom to save his life. You should know before you go through with it."

"Thanks, Boyd. I appreciate the warning."

"I can clean a bathroom," Jett protested.

"Oh, can you? Then I guess you just don't. He also eats oatmeal in his boxers. I'll miss having a roommate, but not that."

"Are you done?"

"Yeah. It's too hot to talk much in here."

I held back a laugh, but I might have let it slip out a little.

Jett tried to look stern, but his eyes sparkled. "Don't encourage him."

"Don't know if you've noticed," Boyd said, "but I don't require encouragement."

"You eat oatmeal?" I asked Jett.

He grinned. "Not since I moved away from my mom."

"Yeah," Boyd said. "I was just trying to make him look good. He's more of a sugar cereal kinda guy."

"I'll still take him." I found Jett's hand in the water, and he squeezed it. "Sugar cereal and all."

⚘

"Conan," I said, edging toward the pup, "put down the shoe."

He backed into the corner, my white wedding shoe clamped between his tiny jaws. Why Boyd had brought him today of all days was beyond me.

I crouched. "If you ruin my shoe, Boyd is going to pay."

"What's wrong?" Boyd called from the front room.

"Conan's about to eat my wedding shoe."

Boyd's voice was full of unhelpful cheer. "He's terrible with shoes. For such a little guy, he can destroy them with a vengeance."

"If I have to drive to the city for new ones before tomorrow, you're going to be sorry," I warned.

Boyd finally appeared. "Drop it, Conan."

Miraculously, Conan dropped the shoe. I snatched it up and examined it—a small chew mark on the inside, but nothing anyone would see.

Conan barked proudly and trotted to Boyd like he'd saved the day.

"Good boy," Boyd said, scooping him up. "I should probably take him home."

"Don't let him eat Jett's tux or anything."

"I think Jett hid it in the closet. He learned his lesson after Conan used his uniforms as a litter box."

"Thanks for dropping by," I said, praying they really left. I wasn't in any mood to replace anything before tomorrow.

"Sure thing. I'll see you tomorrow."

He left with Conan over his shoulder, and I sank onto the couch with relief. *Why can't tomorrow come faster?*

I picked up my phone and called Jett. He'd gone home to change, and we hadn't talked about what we would do after.

"Hey, Ivs."

"Conan chewed on my wedding shoe."

"Sounds about right. Do you want to go get new ones? We have time."

"No. It's fine. I want you to come cuddle on the couch and watch a movie."

"I am one hundred percent in for that. I'll be over in a few."

I tossed my phone to the other side of the couch and waited.

When he arrived, he had a bag of chips. Odd choice, but totally on brand for Jett.

He scooted in next to me. "What are we watching?"

"Something I don't have to think hard to enjoy."

"I hear you. It's been one of those weeks." He popped open the chips and draped one arm across my shoulders. We picked a show, and I leaned in to him. He rested his head on mine. It only took a minute before the chip crunching against my head drove me crazy.

I moved over a little and grinned. "You are a loud cruncher."

He stuck a chip in my mouth. "Crunch with me."

"You're so weird," I said through my mouthful of chips.

He just smiled.

Halfway through the movie, his phone alarm chimed. "Time to go."

I raised an eyebrow. "Go where?"

"To my house."

"The movie isn't even over."

"Doesn't matter. The alarm went off. That means we go."

I shook my head, laughing. "You're ridiculous." But I followed him anyway. Whatever he was planning, he clearly wasn't about to explain.

Chapter 17

The street Jett lived on was full of parked cars. I pretended not to notice, even as my heart raced. Whatever he was up to, this had to be it.

We pulled into the driveway and walked into the living room.

"Surprise!" a wave of voices chorused.

Women from the town were packed into the room, which was decorated in pink-and-gold streamers and balloons.

"Wow," I said, smiling at all the faces. I hated being the center of attention, but these people had welcomed me into town... and I wasn't even sure I knew all of them.

"We've been planning this forever!" Barbra bustled over and hugged me tight. "Every woman should get a wedding shower. Sorry it's so close to the actual event, but we wanted your mom to be here."

My mom waved from where she was chatting with Carol and Tania. I hadn't even told my parents Tania was in town, but it looked like they'd figured it out.

"Well, sit down," Opal said. "Right there in the middle."

Great. They'd planted a chair right in the center of all the folding chairs someone had hauled in. Perfect spot for everyone to stare at me.

"Get another chair for Jett," Opal added.

"No, no," Jett said. "I delivered Ivy. That was my job."

"Oh, come on." Barbra dragged another chair beside mine. "Sit."

I smiled and tugged Jett's hand, pulling him down with me.

"Showers are for women to mingle," he protested.

"That's old-fashioned," Barbra shot back, fluffing her pink hair.

"But there aren't any other guys here."

"Just sit, and we'll feed you."

He chuckled. "Better be good."

"It will be. Opal makes a killer chicken salad sandwich."

"I really do," Opal said, holding her chin high.

I caught sight of Danica across the room and tried not to stare. Something about her still bugged me.

"We aren't traditional," Barbra announced. "So no games or awkward stuff. We watch you open presents, eat food, and mingle."

That sounded fine to me. The less attention, the better—though the present part would still be uncomfortable.

"Okay, presents!" Barbra clapped her hands. "You sit, and Livy agreed to carry the presents over."

Livy handed me the first one, and I peeled back the paper to reveal a canister crammed full of... things. Odd gadgets I didn't even have names for.

"That's from me," Carrie said proudly. "All that stuff is weird kitchen gear nobody actually knows what to do with. I put a note on each explaining it."

I held one up. "An egg separator. Definitely never had one of these. Thanks, Carrie."

The next few were more obvious—dish towels, bowls, silverware. All things we'd use.

"This one's mine," Opal announced.

I opened the pink-and-yellow paper. Inside was a box full of yarn in every color imaginable.

"Thanks," I said carefully. I had no clue what I'd ever do with it. I could count on one hand the number of times I'd used yarn as an adult.

"I'm going to teach you to crochet," Opal declared. "You'll be a pro by this time next year. You'll be able to make all your baby's clothes and save a ton of money."

I hoped my smile looked genuine and not like a grimace. Being taught anything by Opal sounded... intense. I was also sure I wasn't going to take the time to make my future children's wardrobes. That sounded tedious.

"You can make Jett some gloves for the cold Kansas winter," Livy teased, eyes sparkling.

"There's something else in there," Opal added. "At the bottom."

I dug through the yarn and handed the skeins to Jett. Finally, I pulled out... a crochet something. A really short purple-and-yellow dress? Maybe?

I held it up, baffled.

"What the heck is it?" Barbra blurted.

Opal rolled her eyes. "Lingerie, of course."

Barbra snorted, and most of the room broke into laughter that they tried to hide behind napkins. The thing was hideous.

"Wow," I said, doing my best. "You made that?"

"Yep. Been crocheting since I was a girl."

I glanced at Jett. He lounged in his chair, arms crossed, with a small grin on his face. At least he wasn't laughing out loud.

Livy handed me a heavy box from my mom. I opened it and immediately choked up. "Gramma Sue's china?"

Mom smiled. "She would want you to have it."

I touched the edge of a plate and remembered them sitting on my grandma's table. "Thanks, Mom." I didn't dare look at Tania. It might be another thing she would be angry about.

We finished with the presents, and Barbra told Jett and me to get some food. We grabbed some, then sat talking with people.

"I hope you two get off on your honeymoon before anyone else gets killed," Opal said. "Ten bucks says you don't."

The room went quiet for a minute.

"I'm sure everything will be perfect," Carol said, coming over and patting my shoulder. People resumed eating and talking. I wished I were as confident about that as she seemed.

Jett finished his food and sat there smiling to himself.

"What is it?" I asked.

His smile grew. "Just thinking about Opal's present. I can't wait to see you wear it."

"I am not wearing that," I whispered.

"You have to. You'll hurt Opal's feelings."

"You can wear it."

He laughed. "Don't tempt me. I'd rock that thing. What if she asks if you used it?"

"I'll tell her yes. I've heard you can use crocheted things to clean with. I'll use it to scrub the bathtub."

"You know why I love this town?" Jett asked.

"Why?"

"People like Opal and Barbra. You don't get the tight-knit community in the city."

"So we're here for life?" I asked, taking his hand.

"I hope so," he said, giving it a squeeze.

"I know I said no awkward games or anything," Barbra said, "but I think the two of you should tell everyone when you first knew you were interested in each other."

Jett smiled. "I knew the second I saw her peek out the kitchen window at the diner with her hair net and flour-covered apron."

"You did not," I protested.

"I didn't know you were going to fall ridiculously in love with me, but I knew I wanted to get to know you."

I bumped him with my knee. "I am ridiculously in love with you."

People awwed, and I felt sappy. I couldn't believe I'd said that in front of the entire town.

"What did you think the first time you met him?" Livy asked. My mouth turned up. "That I wished I wasn't wearing a hairnet while meeting the hottest guy in Kansas."

"Don't make me blush," Jett teased. "I have a reputation, you know."

"He did insult me the first time we met," I said. "But I got over it fast."

He turned to me. "Insulted you how?"

"That's classified." I couldn't believe I'd said that.

"Oh, I'm worried about it," he said.

I smiled and patted his cheek. "It wasn't bad. I was just nervous about being in a new place."

"Okay, first kiss," Opal said. "If we're being embarrassing, I want to hear that."

My lips pursed together. Our first kiss had been embarrassing, and I still felt it when I thought about it.

Jett smiled and put his hand on my back. "The Clementses' house. We catered for their party."

"I remember that," Livy said. "You all got snowed in."

"Yeah," Jett said, "and Ivy couldn't stop finding herself under the mistletoe."

"It was above the island I was working at! You make it sound like I did it on purpose."

He laughed. "Not the first time, I'm sure. You'd think she would have figured it out after José, Boyd, and Anton all came in and kissed her, but nope."

"Anton kissed you?" Livy bristled.

"On the hand."

She deflated. "Oh, okay."

"And José and Boyd on the cheek." I needed to make sure that was clear.

"But not Jett, I'm guessing," Barbra said.

"Of course not," Jett said. "I'd been waiting a long time for something like that to happen. I figured I had to make it memorable."

"It was." I hoped we could move on now.

"How did Ivy react?" Opal asked.

"Can we change the subject?" I pleaded.

"I want to hear," my mom said.

Jett's grin got bigger. "I tried to pull away. Didn't want to scare her or anything, but she wasn't letting go."

"Oh my heck," I said, covering my cheeks. "They don't need to know any of this."

"Sure we do," Barbra said. "That's what being friends means."

"She got super embarrassed," Jett said. "She was so flustered she went right back under the mistletoe."

"That's enough," I muttered.

He rubbed my back. "Good times."

"How about the second kiss?" Opal asked. "Those are sometimes as good as first kisses."

"No," I protested. "This is done."

"Besides," Jett said, "I'm not sure what counts as the second kiss. Do the mistletoe kisses count as one or two?" he asked, looking at me. "I mean, there was a break between them, but not much. The second might be the one in the closet."

"Oh my heck, Jett. Why are you telling them this?"

"In the closet?" Barbra burst out laughing. "You two beat all."

"We were hiding because..." I sighed. "There's no way to make it sound normal."

Barbra shook her head, still laughing. "That's the story of your entire relationship."

"It really is."

The shower took forever to die down, and I was happy to be finished. I stayed to help Jett clean up. I stuffed wrapping paper into a garbage bag and smiled when I thought of the people in the town.

"How did I insult you?" Jett asked, pulling out the vacuum.

"You didn't really."

"No, I know you. What was it?"

I smiled. "You told me I looked like Tania."

"I hate to tell you this, Ivs, but you do. Why would you care? Tania's pretty."

My eyes narrowed. "Is she now?"

"Come on. You win out on personality, and I was never attracted to Tania. Not even for a second."

"We don't look the same at all. She has dark hair."

He raised his eyebrow. "Your faces have a similar look. I'm not saying you're twins or anything, but there are some similarities."

"I guess I can live with that."

He laughed. "Good, because I don't think you have a choice."

I tied the bag shut and tossed it next to another one.

"You should go home," Jett said, ditching the vacuum and giving me a hug. "Tomorrow's a big day."

I smiled and rested against him. "I can't wait."

Chapter 18

I should be in bed. I didn't want to be tired for the wedding, but lying in my bed staring at the ceiling hadn't gotten me to sleep. I paced the living room, wishing I could push a button and turn off my brain and be asleep.

The apartment was quiet. Tania had moved temporarily into the B&B, so it was just me and Creepers again. At least until tomorrow. My parents were also at the B&B. I would have let them stay here, but they insisted.

A grin spread across my face when I thought of Jett never having to leave to go to his house. "I hope you're going to be nice to Jett," I told Creepers. If I wasn't going to bed, he refused to even pretend. He jumped on the couch and curled up, watching me.

"You need to be nice to Boyd as well. I'll be gone for two weeks. I think you're usually nicer to him than me."

He meowed.

"I'm probably going to trip down the aisle. Who came up with that dumb tradition? I can't imagine anyone wanting an entire church full of people to be staring at them while they try to walk gracefully across the room. Well, maybe Tania. She likes people staring at her."

Creepers blinked.

"I'm sorry. Am I boring you?"

He yawned. I sank down next to him and rubbed his head. He closed his eyes and leaned into me.

A light knock on the door made my head jerk up.

"Who would come at this time?" I whispered. I got up and moved to the window, peeking through the blinds. I sighed and pulled open the door.

Jett grinned guiltily. "I can't sleep. And your light was on."

"You scared me."

"Want to go for a drive?"

"Sure," I said, stepping out into the dark. Everything was quiet and still. We walked down the steps, and it took me until I stepped into the dirt to realize I was barefoot and in my pajamas. I hoped I didn't run into anyone. I climbed into Jett's truck.

"Anywhere you want to drive?" he asked.

"No. I wish I could sleep. I've been pacing and talking to Creepers."

Jett pulled onto the empty street. "I rolled around for a while and decided it wasn't worth it."

"I'm going to fall on my face tomorrow. You know it. Halfway down the aisle. Boyd's going to take pictures, and by noon, it will be all over social media. I'll be the town's new meme."

Jett laughed. "No way. But if you do, I'll pretend to pass out to take the attention off you."

I smiled. "Thanks. Are you nervous?"

"No. Just excited. I mean, I'm not really excited for the boring parts, but I can't wait to be able to say we're married. It feels like I've been waiting a long time. And you have to be a better roommate than Boyd and Conan."

"I wonder why we do all these wedding traditions. Shouldn't they evolve more with time? And why do people want to watch people get married? Weddings are boring. Maybe we should have eloped."

"Our moms would have had something to say about that."

"Probably."

"I've heard horror stories about planning weddings. I'm glad you didn't get crazy."

"I save my crazy for other times."

He chuckled. "Don't I know it."

"I can't be out of control in every aspect of my life."

"I like your type of crazy. Most of the time. I wouldn't mind if you were a little less involved in my job."

"I don't have to be. At least if you're planning on getting a different job. Something a little more boring."

He glanced at me. "I don't see that happening. I figure a little time with Conan will slow you down. He's a needy little thing, and it's your fault I have him."

"I think Boyd wants to keep him."

"He does. I think we should let him. I'll go over every day to clean up after him and take him on a walk. Boyd needs him, but I'm attached. I'm hoping we have a house by the time Boyd can't care for him anymore."

"That sounds nice. We could have just stayed in your house."

"It's too old. I'd rather have something that needs a little less attention."

"Did you see something over there?" I asked, pointing at the auto body shop.

Jett stopped and peered over at the dark building. "What?"

"I thought I saw like a flashlight beam or something inside."

We sat staring at the shop for ten minutes. Nothing.

"I must have imagined it," I said.

"Typical, Ivy."

I turned and gave him a half-hearted glare. "What do you mean?"

He grinned. "Always thinking you see something. You have to admit, you're kind of predictable."

He began driving again.

"I'm not predictable," I protested.

"You totally are."

He stopped at the stop sign, and I reached over and put the truck into park.

"What are you doing?" he asked.

In one smooth motion, I unclicked my seat belt, slid onto his lap, and kissed him. I pulled back. "You didn't predict that."

"And it was totally illegal," he said, kissing me again. "I'd hate to have to arrest you tonight."

"There's no one even awake in town. I doubt it's an issue."

"You're going to be sorry when Ledford pulls us over, and I'm making you explain that one all on your own."

"I'm not scared of Ledford," I said, slipping back into my spot and buckling up.

Jett drove back to the diner, and I frowned. I still didn't feel like I would go to sleep.

"That was short," I said, as he turned off the truck.

He turned and gave me a mischievous smile. "I'm pretty sure the signal you've been sending me is that you wanted me to pull over and kiss you."

I leaned back and smiled. "I wasn't sending you any signals."

"You freaking climbed over here and kissed me. In the middle of the road."

"You call that a signal? That was a flashing neon sign. You don't catch my signals."

He reached over and clicked my seat belt. "Ten minutes, then we'd better go to bed, or we aren't even going to remember tomorrow."

"Ten minutes? You're giving me a time limit? I could go to bed now. I don't need ten minutes of kissing." I really did, but he didn't need to know that.

He sighed. "Well, I might."

"Fine, but I'm only doing it for you." I slid across the seat, glad his truck wasn't fancy enough to have bucket seats. Jett caught me before I'd even settled, one arm wrapping around me like he'd been waiting for this all night. His smile brushed against my mouth before he kissed me.

My brain short-circuited. Clearly, I was more tired than I thought. I pulled away, resting my forehead against his. "You'd better catch me if I trip tomorrow."

"Oh, you're going to trip."

"You're supposed to say I won't."

"But you will. You'll look fabulous when you do it, though."

"Thanks a lot."

"You look tired." He brushed a strand of hair behind my ear.

"I am. It just hit me."

"Go up to bed. I love you."

I kissed him softly. "I love you." I opened the door and climbed down.

"Oh, and Ivy?"

I turned.

"Nice pajamas."

I glanced down at my plaid flannel bottoms and bare feet. "Well, I was going for bridal chic."

I hurried up the steps and into the apartment. Creepers was where I left him, a slight glare on his face, like I'd abandoned him for hours instead of minutes.

"Miss me, buddy?"

He yawned, and I picked him up. "We're done talking about tripping down the aisle. We're going to bed and having good dreams. Deal?" I placed him at the foot of my bed and climbed under the comforter.

I took a deep breath and smiled. My life had been pure chaos since I came to Muddy Creek, and it was still the best part of my life so far. Even if I fell on my face tomorrow, I was looking forward to it. I closed my eyes and fell asleep.

Chapter 19

"You really want to wear your hair down?" Mom asked, curling a strand for me as I sat on the bathroom stool.

I nodded. "Positive."

"Most people wear it up."

"I look better with it down, and since I'm not using a veil, it makes sense to me."

"Alright." She gave the curl a final twist and let it fall. My mom was always good at giving her opinion and then letting me choose. That was probably why we got along so well.

She adjusted the little flower clip in my hair, then stepped back. "Are you nervous?"

"A little. I hate people staring at me, but I can't wait to be with Jett forever."

Her eyes softened. "He's a good guy. I love the Malones. Dad and I are happy for you."

I smiled at her reflection. "Thanks, Mom."

We fussed over earrings, slipped on shoes, and checked makeup one more time. The room smelled of hairspray and roses, and my stomach kept flipping as if I'd already had wedding cake for breakfast.

When I slipped on my last shoe, it was time. I drew a deep breath, smoothed my skirt, and followed her out to the car. The church wasn't far, but I wasn't risking dirt or a stumble. Not today.

The parking lot was full. We were probably the last ones there. My heart hadn't stopped thumping. I touched one of the small white flowers in my hair.

"You look perfect," Mom told me.

I looked down at my dress. The fitted satin clung close through my hips before flaring out into a soft sweep of fabric, every step making it ripple like water. The lace along the bodice caught the light. With the flowers in my hair and the dress flowing around me, it was exactly what I'd imagined—simple and graceful.

I'd made it so I'd arrive just in time—no room left for panicking. Standing with Dad at the church doors, I tightened my grip on the satin of my dress and drew in a deep breath. Passing out halfway down the aisle was not part of the plan.

Tania pressed a bouquet of pink roses into my hands, gave me a quick smile, then disappeared inside to signal the organist. I'd made her my maid of honor to keep the peace.

The first notes of music filled the air, and goose bumps swept across my arms. This was it.

I took Dad's arm, and he kissed my head. "You look beautiful, Ivy girl."

I smiled.

The doors opened, and we walked into the chapel. I could feel all eyes on me as we strolled down the aisle.

My eyes caught Jett's, and he smiled. My heart was so full I thought it might burst. Jett was what happiness looked like, and I was happily walking toward it. I forgot about all the other eyes as I reached him.

A dog barked in the audience. I had no doubt Boyd sat there somewhere with Conan on his lap. That was fine. A little barking never hurt anything.

I handed the bouquet to Tania, then almost panicked when I realized I didn't know what to do now that we were standing in front of the minister. Were we supposed to link arms? I had no clue. I'd never paid attention to weddings because I was usually bored.

My pulse thundered. The chapel smelled like old wood, and every tiny sound—the creak of the pews, the shuffle of shoes, Conan's little bark—seemed magnified.

Jett took my hand, deciding for both of us. Relief loosened my shoulders. He looked steady and calm, which was exactly what I needed. I set my other hand on his arm because it felt natural—and maybe a little possessive—but right then, I didn't care. I wasn't just marrying Jett. I was marrying the one person who made Muddy Creek feel like home.

The minister began talking, and I tried to listen, but my mind kept circling back to Jett and how he was finally, truly going to be mine.

I managed my vows without tripping over the words, and my hand only trembled slightly as we exchanged rings.

When the minister said we could kiss, I suddenly wished we'd discussed what kind of kiss it should be.

Jett leaned down, his lips warm and steady against mine—soft but firm enough to banish every worry. When he pulled back, his smile held nothing teasing, only tenderness.

"I love you," he whispered.

I smiled so hard my cheeks hurt. "I love you."

We relocated to the fellowship hall in the basement for a reception and dance. I felt like I was moving through a dream. I hadn't tripped or even come close. People congratulated us, and I managed to respond.

Conan ran around people's feet, and I wondered if someone would throw him out. Boyd plowed through the crowd trying to catch him.

The cake stood in the corner. José had made the cake a little differently so it wouldn't bring back... other memories.

I shook my head. I wasn't thinking of that. Not today.

People began dancing, and Jett expertly guided me to the dance floor.

"You okay?" he asked.

"Perfect."

"Yes, you are."

I put my arms around him and leaned my head on his chest. I never knew I could feel this happy. I wasn't sure if we were dancing or just hugging and swaying slightly. I could feel Jett's steady heartbeat.

We took a small break to take pictures, then we cut the cake. This was another thing I wasn't excited for. Everyone staring... and I'd forgotten to threaten Jett if he tried smashing the cake on me.

I didn't have to worry. Jett placed it softly in my mouth, and I did the same to him, then he kissed me, the taste of vanilla from the cake still on my tongue.

People clapped.

"Should have smashed it for entertainment," Opal called out from somewhere in the crowd.

"Nope." Jett shook his head. "That's not the tone I want for the rest of our marriage. I respect Ivy too much."

"Cheesy," Boyd declared.

"Some of us like cheese," I said.

Jett laughed. "Good."

I rubbed his cheek. "I almost can't stand how much I love you."

He kissed me again, then pressed his head to mine. "I love you."

I looked around the room and smiled at all the people here to support us. Even some people from Arizona had made it to Kansas. Brian stood near the back, smiling proudly when our eyes met. He lifted a hand in a little wave, like he wasn't sure if he was allowed to interrupt. Seeing him there warmed me more than I expected.

He came over and squeezed my hand. "Congratulations, Ivy. You deserve every good thing." He shook Jett's hand, then he vanished back into the crowd as quietly as he'd arrived.

Tania wore flats, something I never thought I would see. She and Ledford walked up, and we turned to them.

"We're about to head out," she said. "Congratulations. And I actually mean it."

I smiled. Only Tania. "Nice shoes."

She looked down and grimaced. "I'm trying to get used to them."

Ledford put his hand on her back. "I don't care if you wear heels. I'm not insecure."

"I don't want to look like an ogre when I stand by you."

"That could never happen. You look like a model."

Jett and I shared an amused look.

"Aw," Tania said, putting her arms around him. "I don't know how I got so lucky." They started kissing as if we hadn't just been in the middle of a conversation. I grabbed Jett's sleeve and pulled him a fair distance away. They were cute, but in a totally weird, I-don't-need-to-see-this way.

"I'm not sure I'll ever get used to that," Jett said.

I laughed. "I just hope Tania's nice. I've never seen her with a guy when she looked happy and not annoyed. This might be the real thing."

"I'm happy for them."

I was too. And it was good timing. I wondered if it hadn't happened, if Tania would have even come to the wedding. She'd probably still be upset about me falling for Jett.

"You two are welcome to leave whenever you want," my mom said, coming up and giving me a squeeze. "We have plenty of help with cleanup."

"Thanks, Mom."

"It was so beautiful. The entire thing." She hugged Jett, and he patted her shoulder awkwardly.

"Let them go, Candy," my dad said, walking up.

"I wasn't keeping them," she said. "Just telling them goodbye."

We found Jett's parents to let them know we were leaving, then walked out into the parking lot. Jett's truck was decorated with a *Just Married* sign, pink streamers trailing from the bumper. He helped me in, and we drove home.

"We made it, Ivs. No one passed out or died, which is always a positive."

"I can't believe Boyd brought Conan."

He smiled. "It added something."

"I'm just glad he didn't bring Creepers."

Jett pulled off behind the diner and came around to help me out of the truck. The dress didn't make climbing easy. He put his hands on my waist and lowered me. We walked hand in hand up the steps and into the apartment.

Creepers meowed when we entered, but didn't get up from his spot on the couch. Jett closed the door and locked it, which felt like the signal that our new life was beginning. He wrapped his arms around my waist and picked me up off my feet, kissing me.

He set me down, his lips never leaving mine.

For the first time in a while, the town felt safe, and the world felt calm. I knew it wasn't true, but I was going to let the illusion stay with me for now. Tomorrow might bring chaos, but today was ours.

Chapter 20

Jett could sleep for an annoying amount of time, and I couldn't move because his arm had me trapped. My right leg had gone numb, my nose itched, and Creepers stared at me from the foot of the bed like he expected me to break free and feed him. Sure, I could've pushed Jett's arm off, but then I'd feel guilty for disturbing him. What kind of wife would that make me?

The sun shone in the window, and it was after nine. There was no way he usually slept this long. He started work early most days. Maybe knowing he could sleep in made him sleep more deeply.

I rolled over so I was facing him, and his eyes opened to slits.

"Morning," he mumbled, pulling me closer.

I rested my head against him. "I thought you were going to sleep until tomorrow."

"Thought about it. I've been in and out for a while."

"I've been trying to be polite and let you sleep."

He chuckled, his voice rough with sleep. "You don't need to do that. Just kick me over."

"I don't feel like kicking you," I said, kissing the scruff on his chin.

"We have two days until we leave. What do you want to do?"

"Hmm. I don't know. What about you?"

"I'm all set for being lazy. I say we sit around in pajamas for two days eating junk food and watching TV."

"That sounds good for about two hours."

"Two and a half, tops. Then we open presents."

"Fifteen more minutes."

"It's something."

"We could at least take Creepers for a walk."

Jett cracked one eye open. "You want to put that cat on a leash?"

"Fine. I'll walk. You and Creepers can sit here and perfect your lazy routine."

He groaned dramatically. "I can walk if I have to."

"You're hopeless."

"Don't worry." He tucked me against him again. "I'll keep you thoroughly entertained for the entire two days."

He kissed me softly, then we both jumped when there was a knock on the door. Jett climbed out of bed. "I've got it."

I sat up and pushed my hair back. Then my eyes widened, and I hopped out of bed. "Jett! Don't answer the door in your pajama bottoms!"

Too late. He was opening the door. I closed the bedroom door so it was only open a crack and listened. It was my dad and Jett's dad delivering the presents. Lovely. I closed the door and hurried into the bathroom for a quick shower.

When I was ready for the day, I went out and found a pile of presents in the middle of the living room. Jett stood in the kitchen making breakfast.

He looked up from the frying pan and grinned. "Good news. Your dad didn't seem traumatized by my pajama bottoms."

"Don't you own a robe?" I asked.

"Yeah, but it's too warm, and still at my house."

I tilted my head. "Great. So your big contribution to our new life together is public indecency?"

He laughed. "You can go get me a shirt if it makes you feel better."

"Too late for that."

"I thought you'd be happy I wasn't in my boxers."

"Are you making Spam?"

"Limited cooking skills, remember? If you make it crispy, it's good."

"I'm not complaining. It was in my cupboard." I sat at the table and yawned. It was weird not to have anywhere to be.

Jett placed a plate of scrambled eggs on the table and another of Spam. Very well cooked. We sat quietly eating. It was a new thing to wake up and eat with someone. Jett was right. The Spam was slightly burned.

We cleaned up after breakfast, then went out to the couch to open presents.

Jett smiled. "I wonder if Opal made anything."

"Oh my heck," I muttered, leaning into his arms. "That was embarrassing."

"And you didn't even wear it."

"And I never will."

"Opal's going to teach you to crochet. That sounds exciting."

"As exciting as watching paint dry. I hope she forgets."

He pulled me onto his lap and kissed me. "Marriage agrees with me."

I laughed. "All twenty hours of it?"

"You want to take turns opening presents or just start ripping things apart?"

"Take turns."

"That will take a while."

I scooted back to the couch and picked up the guest book that was on top. "I'm going to have to go through this. A lot of yesterday felt like I was in a daze."

"Presents first."

I opened a set of tools.

"Power tools," Jett said. "Nice."

He opened some lace doilies. "Do people still use these things? I bet they're from my mom. She puts them under everything."

We finished with the presents, and Jett went to take a shower. I opened the guest book and scanned over the names. Just like I thought, some people had come that I hadn't remembered seeing.

I rested my head against the couch and squinted to make out all the signatures. On the bottom of the third page, I stopped and sucked in a breath. "McKay Hayes?" I muttered. "Are you kidding me?"

I stared at the name until my eyes burned, then I popped up and ran to the bathroom door and pounded on it. "Jett!"

The water turned off. "Yeah?"

"Hayes's first name is McKay?"

"What? Hang on a minute."

I stood there breathing hard. I knew something was off about Hayes.

The door opened, and Jett came out with dripping hair and a towel around his waist. "What's wrong?"

I held up the guest book. "Hayes. His first name is McKay. Did you know that?"

"I'm sure I did at some point, but I didn't remember."

"That means he's connected to the smugglers! Remember the receipt?"

Jett combed his fingers through his hair. "Maybe, but it could still be the McKay brothers. I trust Hayes, and he was working on the smuggling case. That receipt could mean anything."

I rubbed my lips together as I thought. "He was in the woods, Jett. Right where the jewels were hidden. That's not a coincidence."

"Because he was on the case."

"Why weren't you working that case?"

"Ledford and Hayes had it under control."

I took a deep breath and let it out through my nose.

Jett pulled me into a hug. "We aren't going to have a lazy two days, are we? I see it in your eyes. You have your mystery face on."

"Can't we at least talk to Hayes? I don't want to ruin your plans, but just for a few minutes?"

He kissed my head. "My plans were default plans. Not important. I'm not sure I feel like asking one of my deputies, who I have a really good relationship, if he's part of a smuggling ring."

"Just ask why the smugglers would have a receipt with his name. And if he knew where some of the jewels were stashed, why did he leave them there?"

"So no one would realize he was onto them?"

It made sense, but I wanted more closure than the case had. "Your hair's dripping on me."

He released me. "We can make a plan. Hayes is patrolling the smaller towns this morning, so we can't talk to him until this afternoon."

"Fine with me." I moved a piece of his hair. "You should probably talk to him without me. If I'm there, I'll just look like the crazy woman."

He grinned. "When has that ever stopped you?"

"I have some restraint."

"Do you?"

Creepers yowled from the couch as if he were answering for me. Jett raised a brow.

"See? Even the cat doesn't buy it," he said.

I grabbed the guest book and held it up again. "Fine. But if Hayes is innocent, he's still got explaining to do."

"Because his name is McKay? I don't think he was hiding that."

"Okay, I'm losing it."

"Can we try to forget about it for a while?"

"I guess I can try. It's hurting me."

"I see that." He ran his finger over the side of my face. "The vein on the side of your head is throbbing. You want to run out and try to arrest Hayes with absolutely no authority."

"That passed after I calmed down a little and realized how hot you are with wet hair." He put his hands on my waist and smiled. "I'll remember that." I kissed him, trying to ignore the guest book waiting on the table. For now, I'd let myself enjoy this moment—but I wasn't done with Hayes. Not even close.

He pulled back. "You're thinking about Hayes."

"Sorry."

"I thought I could hold your attention longer than a day."

I smiled and hugged him. "It's off my mind. You have all my attention."

His arms tightened around me, his voice warm against my ear. "Good. Because you've got all of mine."

Then his next kiss left no room in my heart or my head for anything but him.

Chapter 21

I peeked out the window, hoping to see Jett. He'd left over an hour ago, and I'd thought it would be a quick talk with Hayes and then be over. No sign of him. I picked up the small piece of paper with a phone number I'd found in the kitchen and stared at it.

Calling it was weird. It could be anything. It wasn't like the killer had taken time to scribble down a number. I dialed it and waited.

"Hello?" a woman said.

"Uh, hi…"

"Ivy? Do you need something?"

"Livy?"

"Yeah."

I sighed. "Why is your phone number written on one of the canisters in the kitchen?"

"What...? Oh. Uh... I was going to clean that off. When I started dating Anton, he lost his contact list, and I was in a hurry, so I scribbled it down so he could get it later. Sorry. I'll clean it the next time I'm in."

"It's fine. I just wanted to make sure it wasn't related to anything shady."

"Nope. Sorry."

My eyes narrowed when I spotted Hayes out the window. He was walking on the sidewalk across the street.

I ended the call and hurried through my apartment and out the door, barely taking time to let each foot land on a step.

I ran around the corner and watched him. He moved at a steady pace, and it would be hard to follow him without making it obvious. I walked quickly down my side of the street and hoped he didn't look over.

He stopped in front of a boarded-up shop on the square. Old wooden planks covered the windows, and the place had long since been abandoned. Hayes tried the knob, glanced around once, and slipped inside.

My heart thumped. I jogged across the street, stopping in front of the building. With the windows sealed, I couldn't hear a thing. I hesitated a moment, then reached for the knob. The door squeaked as it opened, and I slipped inside.

A musty smell entered my nose, and I frowned. Some of these old buildings needed to come down. No one was going to use them. They weren't safe, and they weren't cared for. I slid into the room and shut the door. Hayes had to be in here somewhere.

I took a quiet step forward, and suddenly, a firm arm wrapped around my waist and a hand covered my mouth. I tried to scream or bite, but the hand was pressed too tightly. I stomped on his foot, and he barely grunted but released me. I took three fast steps forward, then turned to see Hayes.

He looked wary. "Mrs. Malone, you're going to get me fired."

My heart was thundering, but something in me still liked hearing Mrs. Malone. "Maybe you need to get fired."

"Why do you keep following me?"

"Did you talk to Jett?"

His eyes narrowed. "Not since yesterday."

"He went to talk to you. That was over an hour ago."

He pulled out his phone. "I missed his call. I've been busy."

"Doing what?"

"It's classified."

"When I was trapped in the smuggler's shed. There was a receipt in there with your name on it. Why is that?"

He rubbed his chin. "What kind of receipt?"

"I couldn't make it out."

"Great. And now the sheriff thinks I'm up to something?"

190

"No, he thinks highly of you. I think you're up to something."

"Was there a blue backpack by chance?"

"Yeah, there was."

"I lost that bag in the woods a few weeks ago. It was careless of me, but I bet Levi and his men took it. From the way you're glaring at me, I'm guessing you think I was working with Levi?"

I shrugged. "I'm undecided."

"That's why you ran the other day in the woods."

"You were chasing me."

"Only to ask why you were there. I was going to warn you it wasn't safe, but I guess you figured that out on your own."

"Why are you here?" I demanded, like I was the cop and not the other way around.

"Come here," he said, going into the next room. Following him was probably stupid, but I did it anyway.

The room was full of crates, and it smelled moldy.

"What's in the crates?" I asked. "Surely not jewelry. And they look old."

"These crates were full of stolen car parts. Like a long time ago. Two sheriffs before Sheriff Malone. That case was cracked. I'm not sure why they left the crates. This place belongs to a guy who went to prison."

I blinked. "Okay...?"

"I thought I saw someone come in here one night, but I was going to an emergency, and I couldn't stop. Something isn't complete about the jewelry case, and I wonder if there might be something hiding in this place."

"Do you think Levi killed Elias?"

"No idea, but I think we might be missing someone." He smiled slightly. "From the way you're looking at me, I'm guessing you think it's me."

"I saw you get the jewelry in the tree and look at it."

He pulled a folded paper out of his back pocket and opened it. "This is a map I made of the woods. See all the x's?"

"Yeah?"

"Those are places I found stashes. I didn't take them. I just marked where they were. I didn't want anyone knowing we were onto them yet."

It made sense. Maybe I'd been wrong.

"Why would Ledford hide caches in the same area where smugglers were working?"

He shrugged. "Ledford's helped me some, but it's my case. I never took him to that area, so he didn't know that was the spot the smugglers were working. I should have communicated better with him."

"That makes more sense."

"I can't stop, though," Hayes said. "Not until I feel like all the loose ends have been tied up."

"I think it's odd there aren't any clues from the murder."

"Nothing but the weird cut on Elias's neck."

Jett hadn't told me about a weird cut.

"Did you see it?" I would let him think I knew about it.

"Yeah."

"I might like to solve mysteries, but I don't like to stare at dead bodies. I didn't get a good view of it."

"I get that."

"What did it look like?"

"The cut was right at the side of his neck. Not deep enough to kill him, but it stood out. Almost like someone grabbed him, and jewelry or something sharp dug in."

He moved over to a crate. "This one isn't as dusty as the others." He pried it open and smiled. "Bingo."

I looked in to see several small boxes that looked like the one I'd thought was a geocache.

"The day after we arrested Levi, we went back to pick up all of the boxes of jewelry, and most of them were already gone. That was another reason I was sure someone else was involved."

"Could it be Danica?"

He looked up at me, then back in the crate. "What would make you think that?"

"She was involved with all the guys at Levi's shop, and she delivers things. What if she was helping them move things?"

"I've had that thought a few times, but no evidence to go with it."

"You should question her."

He sighed. "I try to avoid her, but yeah, maybe." Hayes picked up a box and opened it, the jewelry shining up at him. "I'm going to call Ledford and tell him about this. We need to take it before someone comes back for it."

He called Ledford, and I studied the room.

I felt like Hayes was telling the truth, but I would stay until Ledford came, just to make sure he didn't take off with the crate.

"Sounds like you have skills," I said.

Hayes shrugged. "I'm good at what I do."

"Do you like your job?"

He paused. "Not really."

"Then why do it?"

"What else am I qualified for? I would do something else in a heartbeat if I could. My dad was a cop, and so were both of my grandpas. It just seemed like the thing to do."

"You're young. You can change careers."

He shrugged. "I don't hate my job. I just don't love it."

Ledford came in and looked around. "The city shouldn't leave all these empty old buildings sitting here waiting for trouble."

"Seriously," Hayes agreed.

"I'd better go," I said, not sure how to dismiss myself for trespassing. I went out, and Jett was coming from the other direction. I hurried over to him.

"What are you doing?" he asked me.

I smiled. "Bugging some of your officers."

"Which ones? I can't find Hayes."

"I was just with him." I told him everything Hayes had told me.

"See? I told you. He's a good guy."

"You left things out when you told me about things. You never told me Elias had a scratch on his neck."

"I didn't figure you needed to know."

I glared playfully at him. "If you keep things from me, I'm going to have to snoop harder."

"Please don't. I'd hate to have to arrest my wife."

"And I'd hate to be arrested, so tell me things."

"Legally, there are things I can't tell you. I have to follow the rules to the best of my ability, and you make that really hard."

"You love it." I wrapped my arms around his neck.

"Maybe, but I'll never admit it." He leaned down and kissed me.

"Public street!" Boyd yelled, pulling us apart. "As the mayor, I declare that there is no kissing in the street. It's a hazard, and no one wants to see it."

"You know I'm letting you live in my house until it sells, right?" Jett asked.

Boyd crossed his arms. "Are you trying to threaten me? No kissing, no threats. Public street ordinance."

"Boyd..." Jett patted him on the shoulder. "You need more hobbies."

"Darn right I do."

Jett grinned. "Maybe Opal can teach you to crochet."

"She tried once about seven years ago. It's a good thing that woman never became a teacher because she takes every mistake you make personally."

We all laughed and moved out of the street.

"You two just got married. What are you doing standing in the street?"

"We were kissing," Jett reminded him, "but you ruined that."

"You have your own place. Spare the neighbors."

I linked my fingers with Jett's and turned to Boyd. "Are you sure you can watch Creepers while we're gone?"

"Positive. Creepers and Conan love me. We're going to have a great time."

Normally, I'd ask Brian to watch Creepers—he had a way with the little rascal. But Brian was still off in Nebraska. He'd come for the wedding but left right after.

We said goodbye to Boyd, then went back up to the apartment.

"Do you need to go help Hayes and Ledford?" I asked. I didn't want him to, but I also didn't want to keep him from his job if something needed doing.

"No. They've been working this case, and I trust them. I'm off duty and staying out of everything that you'll let me."

"I don't push you into things. Do I?"

"Occasionally."

"Alright. Two and a half weeks, and no investigating anything."

He pulled me back to the couch. "I'll believe that when I see it."

"What do you want to do?" I asked. "There's still a lot of day left."

"I want to do what you want to do."

"Give me options."

"We could have an *X-Files* marathon, or we could spend an hour or two making out on the couch."

"I'm not watching *X-Files*. My dad was obsessed with it when I was a kid, and I hated it."

"Then it's been decided. And let me just say, you made the right choice."

"I always do."

Chapter 22

I was so sick of hearing crashes in the kitchen. José wouldn't be in yet, so that meant whoever was down there probably shouldn't be. I listened for another minute and didn't hear anything.

I knocked on the bathroom door. Jett was going to think he had just signed up to have no private bathroom time after today.

"Yeah?"

"Something crashed downstairs. I'm going to go check."

"No, no, no. Wait for me."

I waited a minute, and he came out. "I'm going to get a soundproof bathroom so I can't hear when you come pounding on the door."

I smiled. "Sorry."

He grabbed his gun from the dresser and went to the door in the bedroom that led to the diner. "Stay here."

"No way."

He sighed and checked the safety on his gun before opening the door. I quietly followed him. I could hear something down there, but I wasn't sure what. A scrape. A thump. Then... a giggle? That didn't make sense.

Jett got to the bottom and peeked around the wall. "Seriously?" he said, going around the corner.

Tania and Ledford stood in the middle of the diner looking guilty.

"Do either of you have a key?" he asked.

Tania nodded. "I'm helping with the diner while Ivy's gone."

"And you thought you should come in at six in the morning for some lip action? You have a place."

"Uhh..." Ledford said. "Tania needed help getting the kitchen ready."

"José will be here in thirty minutes."

Tania put her hands on her hips. "You could've given us thirty more minutes of privacy. But no, Sheriff Killjoy strikes again."

"You can't make out in the diner," I said. "It's... not sanitary."

"Please," Tania said. "I bet you and Jett have."

I couldn't swear to it one way or the other. I honestly couldn't remember.

"I hope you aren't going to make a habit of this while we're gone," I said.

"I should go," Ledford said.

Tania glared at him. "No. We still have thirty minutes. Let's go out back." She turned, and I saw something on her arm, right below her sleeve.

"What happened to your arm?" I asked, walking closer. She had an odd, jagged cut.

Tania turned and reached back, touching it.

"One of those jerks who abducted us cut me with his stupid ring."

Jett leaned in. "Let me see."

She moved her hand.

"That looks like the cut that was on Elias."

I sucked in a breath. "One of the smugglers was the killer. But which one?"

"No one we took in had a ring on."

"He had it on his pinky," Tania said. "Big ugly silver thing. I think he actually felt bad when it started bleeding. That's when Kaz started trying to punch everyone so we could escape."

My eyes darted around as I tried to think.

"What is it?" Jett asked.

"It was Oliver."

Jett shifted and crossed his arms. "Oliver? He was the only one not getting illegal money from Levi."

"Let me talk to Levi."

"That sounds like a terrible idea."

I grabbed Jett's hand and pulled him to the door, leaving the others to... get ready for the morning rush, or whatever they were going to do.

"I can't just let you interrogate Levi."

"How do you decide when you're going to let me do things?" I asked, dragging him along.

"Part of it is how tired I am. Or how distracting you are when you want something."

I led him straight to the sheriff's office. We went in and found one deputy at the desk. He must have had the night shift.

"We're just going to talk to Levi for a minute," Jett told him.

He yawned and nodded.

We went back to the long hallway with a few cells. Levi sat on his bed, glaring as the light shone in. His beard was even more matted than usual.

"Why didn't you pay Oliver for helping with the smuggling?" I asked.

He rubbed his eyes. "What are you talking about?"

"Oliver was helping you. Why weren't you paying him?"

"He wasn't helping. He had nothing to do with it."

"You're lying. Why? You two didn't get along. Why protect him?"

He scratched his greasy head. "He wasn't with us."

"We know he was."

Levi just stared. And so did Jett.

"The night Elias died. What happened?"

He groaned. "Why do we have to go over this so many times? I needed to get something from the diner."

"The key?"

"Yeah. I knew I lost it there, and I couldn't have anyone find it. Something came up, so I sent Elias instead."

"Did Oliver know you were going to go to the diner?"

"Yep."

"Did he know Elias went instead?"

Levi's eyes went wide. "No."

I nodded and turned to Jett. "Oliver straight out told me if he was going to kill someone, it would have been Levi. He was mad because Levi told them they couldn't hang out with Danica anymore. I bet he went to kill Levi. He messed up and killed Elias."

Levi ran a hand over his pale face. "I can't believe it."

"Why are you trying to protect him?" I asked.

"Oliver comes across as a good guy, but he's worse than the rest of us. I saw him break someone's finger once, just because he was having a bad day. He wanted to be paid in cash so there would never be a trail back to him. I can't have him knowing I said anything about him."

"I'm going to grab Ledford and go check out Oliver's house." Jett turned to me. "Is that okay?"

I nodded. "Just try to be fast."

We stepped outside, and Jett jogged to his truck.

He pulled out a second later, and I stood on the sidewalk once again.

Danica's van stopped in front of me, and she got out. "Hi, Ivy. Can we talk?"

"Uh… sure."

She sat on the curb, so I sat next to her.

"You and Sheriff Malone inspired me."

I blinked. "Oh?"

She looked at her hands. "At your shower, I saw how in love you were. It made me reevaluate my life. I want what you two have. Not whatever mess I've made for myself. I'm just not sure I can find it."

I put my hand on hers. "I'm sure you can."

"I doubt around here. Everyone knows me. And judges me. I get it, but I think my best bet is to go somewhere else."

"It might be," I said honestly.

She nodded. "I need a change anyway. I just wanted to thank you for opening my eyes."

I gave her a small smile. "Good luck with everything."

"Thanks." She stood.

"Oh, Danica?"

"Yeah?"

"Did you help the guys at the auto shop deliver packages?"

She frowned. "Yes. I don't know what was in them. I kind of suspected it was something illegal, but I didn't ask."

"Oh," I said. "One more thing. I heard you tell Hayes you knew what he did. What did he do?"

She frowned. "How did you even hear that? Never mind. He didn't do anything that I know of, but I figured everyone has a secret. Maybe if I said it, he would think I knew something and freak out or something. I'm not proud of any of this."

I nodded, and she left. She sounded sincere, but with Danica, it was hard to know where the performance ended and the truth began.

Oliver's car pulled up to the shop across the street, and I sent Jett a quick text letting him know, then I stood and walked over.

"Hey," Oliver said, smiling.

"Hello." I didn't have a plan.

"Can I help you with something?"

"You're still working the shop even though Levi's in jail?"

He shrugged. "No one ever said not to, so I keep showing up."

"Who's gonna pay you?"

"Levi's going to be put away for a while. I'm hoping he'll let me buy him out."

"Not if you're in jail with him." I admit, my mouth is occasionally faster than my sense.

He smiled. "Excuse me?"

"You heard me. And you're going away longer. Murder is worse than smuggling."

"Murder? Who would I kill?"

"Poor Elias. But you thought he was Levi."

His smile stayed on his lips, but his eyes flickered—just for a second—before he covered it with a laugh.

"My guess?" I said. "You were mad that Levi wouldn't let you hang out with Danica anymore. You knew he was going to the diner. You ran in, whacked him with the frying pan, accidentally scratching him with your ring. Then, oops. It was Elias, not Levi."

He swallowed and gave a nervous laugh. "That's ridiculous."

"But true. You were moving as fast as you could, which was why he was covered in cake. You must have swung so hard you hit the cake and then Elias, then you tore out of there."

He turned to the shop. "I don't have time to waste with you."

"Fine. You can talk to the police."

He paused, then turned and grabbed my arm, yanking me into the shop. I'd only been about 90 percent sure I was right, but now there was no doubt. Also, if I survived this, Jett would be annoyed with me.

Oliver slammed the door and locked it. "Look," he said, "you don't need to tell anyone about this. Everyone can agree Levi is rotten. It sucks that I got Elias by accident, but he wasn't a great guy either. He was just as deep into smuggling as anyone."

"And it's all because of Danica? The woman who didn't care about any of you."

He rolled his eyes. "No, it's hardly about her at all. That was just the last straw. Levi was hogging most of the money from the smuggling and doing the least amount of work. I was sick of it. I would have handled the entire thing better than he did. Then he was stupid enough to take Ledford and that girl? He had no right to be heading anything."

"And you do?"

"I'm more qualified, yes. And now you've forced my hand. I wish people would stop doing that."

"Hurt me, and you'll just be in more trouble. I'm not the only one who knows."

"You're just trying to worry me."

"No. The police are out looking for you as we speak. And some of them are probably on their way here."

He pushed past me, going out the front door. I turned and chased him, but almost as soon as he was out the door, he ran into Hayes. I'd never been so glad to see curly-haired Hayes in my life. He blocked Oliver's swing like it was nothing and dropped him with a single punch. If I survived this, I might actually trust him. He pulled his gun and aimed.

Jett's truck pulled up, and he ran over with Ledford. Oliver scowled from the ground as he was surrounded. I quickly told them everything that had happened.

"You two have this?" Jett asked.

"Got it," Hayes said.

Jett walked over and held out his hand. His eyes were hard, and I could tell he was holding in his anger. I took his hand, and he led me to his truck and opened the door for me. I got in and buckled up. We drove the short distance to the diner and around the back.

I sat in the truck once Jett stopped and tried to think of what to say.

Jett opened my door for me, and I climbed down. We went up the steps to the apartment and inside.

Creepers meowed and rubbed against my legs. I went and filled his dish, then went out to find Jett on the recliner, his face still serious.

I stood there feeling like a naughty little kid standing in the principal's office.

"Sorry," I mumbled.

He sighed. "Ivs, you're going to give me a heart attack. You can't put yourself in danger all the time."

"I don't mean to."

He held out his hand, and I took it. He pulled me over onto his lap. "Maybe you need a nine-to-five job. Then you'd be too busy to get into trouble."

"I'd probably still manage." I shifted around until I was comfortable in his arms.

"I'm sure you would. Could you at least try not to confront killers when you're alone?"

"I could try."

"You freak me out sometimes."

I grabbed the handle on the chair and reclined it, then cuddled into him. "Don't be mad at me."

"I'm not mad. I was just scared when you sent me that text."

"The bad guys are in jail, and tomorrow, we'll be off on our honeymoon. Two weeks of absolutely no mysteries."

He laughed softly. "That's what you say. We've left Muddy Creek two times, and both times, we ended up in a mess."

"That's true."

He took my hand and put it on his chest. "Feel that? My heart's still not beating normally."

I wrapped my arms around him.

"If I can help it, it will never beat normally again." I kissed him with everything I had, hoping he could feel what he meant to me. I couldn't change who I was, but I could try harder to be the part of me he needed most. He did that for me, so I could do it for him.

Chapter 23

"I can't believe we're doing a geocache search a few hours before our plane takes off," Jett said.

I tugged him by the hand across town. "Ledford worked hard on this. The least we can do is find some of them."

Half the town was running around like it was an Easter egg hunt. Some people had driven out to the caches in the countryside, but we were sticking close so we wouldn't get lost right before our honeymoon.

"Found one!" Boyd called from near the library entrance. He pulled a container out of a potted tree and held it up like buried treasure.

"Which one are we looking for?" Jett asked.

I checked my phone. "The clue says *Near the library, you must wait, look around, and check the gate.*" We walked over to the side gate. "I don't think anything could be hiding here."

Jett scanned the fence and the shrubs. "I have nothing. This really isn't my thing."

I eyed the post next to the gate. "What if it's under the cap?"

Jett chuckled. "I'm not prying that off. Nobody would hide something there."

I climbed a few steps up the fence and popped the cap loose.

"Ivs, don't wreck Brian's fence."

I jumped down and revealed the spider cache glued underneath. "Told you."

"People are nuts," Jett muttered. "Who does stuff like this? I'm surprised I haven't arrested anyone for it."

"Didn't you notice Ledford's shirt?"

"No. Why?"

"It said *Excuse me, Officer, I was just geocaching.* He thinks he's hilarious."

Jett smirked. "Sounds like him."

I slid the spider back into place and secured the cap.

"Where now?" Jett asked.

I handed him the phone. "You choose."

He studied the list, then grinned. "What's the Ivy cache?"

I froze. "What?"

He laughed. "You wanna hear the clue?"

I cocked my head. "I'm not sure."

"She likes to poke, she likes to pry, you might mistake her for a private eye. Go to where she gives us food, look near a bush, and feel the mood."

"Nice, Ledford," I muttered. "It's good he became a cop and not a poet."

"To the diner?"

"Yep." We went over, and I glanced around. "There aren't any bushes. There isn't any dirt. Unless it's in the back."

"Let's check."

We went around, and I tried to remember if there was a bush back there. It was mostly dirt and a big dumpster.

Jett pointed. "There. A bush."

I squinted. "That's not a bush. It's a big weed."

"Closest thing I see to a bush."

I shook my head and went over near the diner wall to where the large weed grew. A box that was hardly hidden sat behind it. Jett pulled it out and opened it. I peeked around him.

"Now that's an Ivy cache," Jett said.

Inside were a magnifying glass, a pair of toy handcuffs, a few pennies, and a small tool for picking locks.

"Ledford probably thinks he's so funny," I said.

"He kind of is."

"Well, I'm taking this." I slipped the tool out.

"Don't you have to put something in to replace it?"

I pulled an unopened lip gloss from my purse and put it inside. "There."

He laughed. "How many more do we have to do?"

"Depends. You wanna win?"

"I've got it," Boyd said. "Stop worrying. It's not like I don't know how to take care of a cat."

I wrinkled my nose. "I just never know what you might do."

He laughed. "That makes two of us."

I put a bag of cat food on the table of Jett and Boyd's house and looked around for anything potentially cat-unfriendly.

"If I need anything, Matt Hooper said he's willing to help. He's already watching most of Brian's cats while he's in Nebraska. He's pretty much an expert."

"Alright," I mumbled. I scooped Creepers up and cuddled him to me. "You be a good boy, alright?"

He meowed in protest and squirmed to get to the floor. He wanted to explore the new area.

"Don't let Conan bug him."

"It's usually the other way around."

Jett came down the stairs with a backpack on his shoulder. "I should have moved all my stuff before we left. Now

I'm going to have to do it when I get home. Are you ready?"

I frowned. "Probably."

"What's wrong?"

"She's worried I won't spoil Creepers enough," Boyd said.

"I doubt that's an issue. He'll probably spoil him sick. I've seen him sneaking the animals things they shouldn't have several times."

I pointed at him. "No sneaking him food, Boyd. If Creepers comes back fat and grumpy, I'm coming for you."

He laughed. "They're going to have the best care."

"They better."

"And I forgot to tell you. My condo will be ready in three weeks, so as soon as you get home, it will almost be time for y'all to move me in."

"That sounds like great fun," Jett said.

"Then you can sell this place."

"Yep."

There was a knock on the door. We all walked over since we were leaving anyway. Ledford stood there.

"Anything wrong?" Jett asked.

I crossed my fingers. No one better ruin my honeymoon.

"It's fine. I just thought you might want to know everything we learned last night. Hayes and I were up all night talking to all the prisoners."

Jett checked his watch. "We have about five minutes."

"Levi's brother wasn't in as deep as the others, and he was willing to spill. According to him, Levi had his fingers in more than just smuggling. Oliver knew it all and told Levi that if he ever went down, he would tell everything. That's why he said Oliver wasn't in on it."

My eyes narrowed. "I knew it. Levi wasn't protecting Oliver. He was scared of him." Okay, I didn't really know it, but I knew something wasn't adding up.

Jett looked at his watch again. "We need to go. Take care while I'm gone."

Ledford nodded. "Everything will be fine. You don't have to worry about Muddy Creek while you're gone."

"Nice geocaching game," I said. "And that bush behind the diner is actually a weed."

"Yeah, well, saying weed would have thrown off my rhyme."

"I bet you think you're clever."

Ledford gave an uncharacteristic grin. "I do."

Tania waved from Ledford's patrol car.

"Why is Tania in your car?" Jett asked, sounding tired.

Ledford shrugged. "You, of all people, are asking me that?"

I smiled and wrapped my arm around Jett's. "He has a point."

He glanced at me. "You weren't controllable. Still aren't."

"Hey, if Tania and Ledford ever get married, you all will be related," Boyd said.

We all stood there for a moment, and I resisted laughing. A year ago, I would have shuddered, but now the idea didn't feel so far-fetched. Maybe Muddy Creek had changed me—or maybe Ledford wasn't quite as terrible as he used to be.

Ledford was scowling, and Jett looked thoughtful.

"We'll see you all," I said, pulling Jett toward my car. We got in, and I smiled. We were on our way to what was going to be the most memorable honeymoon in history. Knowing us, it would be unforgettable for all the wrong reasons.

"You ready for this?" Jett asked.

"I'm ready." He reached for my hand, and I laced my fingers through his as we drove off. If Muddy Creek had taught me anything, it was this: the chaos never stopped. But neither did we.

José's *Cheating* Emergency Wedding Cupcakes

Ingredients

1 box white cake mix

1 cup milk

1/3 cup melted butter

3 eggs

1 tsp vanilla extract

Frosting

1 cup butter, softened

3 cups powdered sugar

1 tsp vanilla

2–3 tablespoons milk

Instructions

Preheat oven to 350°F. Line a muffin pan with 18–24 cupcake liners.

In a large bowl, mix the cake mix, milk, melted butter, eggs, and vanilla until smooth.

Divide the batter into the liners and bake 15–18 minutes or until a toothpick comes out clean.

For the frosting, beat butter until fluffy, then add powdered sugar, vanilla, and milk until smooth.

Frost once the cupcakes are cool.

Also By Kristy Dixon

<u>**Cozy Mystery**</u>
Murder With a Side of Bacon
Murder With a Hint of Cinnamon
Murder With a Fudge Brownie to Go
Murder With a Splash of Vanilla
Murder With a Drizzle of Syrup
Murder With a Slice of Pie
Murder With a Swirl of Blueberry
Murder With a Bite of Biscotti
Murder With a Sip of Eggnog
Suite Lies and Alibis

Not So Suite Caroline
A Suite Case of Murder
Suite Silent Night Secret
Peril Among the Pansies
Murder Among the Moonflowers
Malice Among the Marigolds

<u>Young Adult</u>
The Silver Eclipse (3 books)
The Amethyst Crown
More Than Once Upon a Time
Trapped In Once Upon a Time
The Beginning of Once Upon a Time
Riviand Lost (5 books)

<u>Coming Soon!</u>
Murder With a Crumble of Cookies
Lies Among the Lilies
Marrying My Prickly Boss

About the Author

Kristy Dixon started writing stories at age seven and never stopped. These days, she writes cozy mysteries full of quirky characters, small-town charm, and the occasional dead body. She also writes YA novels when the teens in her head get too loud to ignore. Kristy lives with her husband, kids, one spoiled cat, and a flock of chickens who think they run the place. When she's not writing or wrangling her crew, she's likely playing board games, plotting murders (fictional, of course), or dreaming about cookies.